"I'm staying with you."

Shelly couldn't have heard him right. A man like Matt Collingsworth didn't put himself out for a prospective employee. But then she wouldn't have expected one of the richest men in Texas to be sitting across from her tonight, either.

"What did you say?" she asked.

"You shouldn't be alone until we know why someone tried to kill you today."

"And you're planning to serve as my bodyguard? That isn't necessary."

"Actually, it is. Family tradition, the cowboy code and all that. A real man never walks away from a woman in danger."

He'd walk away fast enough if he knew she was CIA and here to put him and his family away for life. She should be thanking her lucky stars for this entrée into the inner sanctum of the world she'd come to infiltrate. But only one word came to mind. and it seemed to be shouting inside her head and echoing through every cell of her body:

Help!

JOANNA WAYNE

LOADED

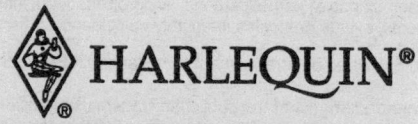

To all my Texas friends who so willingly share their family stories with me. To my husband for putting up with me when I'm so lost in one of my stories I forget to cook dinner or come to bed. And a special thanks to all my readers who love a cowboy tale the way I do.

ISBN-13: 978-0-373-69332-0
ISBN-10: 0-373-69332-X

LOADED

ABOUT THE AUTHOR

Joanna Wayne was born and raised in Shreveport, Louisiana, and received her undergraduate and graduate degrees from LSU-Shreveport. She moved to New Orleans in 1984, and it was there that she attended her first writing class and joined her first professional writing organization. Her first novel, *Deep in the Bayou*, was published in 1994.

Now, dozens of published books later, Joanna has made a name for herself as being on the cutting edge of romantic suspense in both series and single-title novels. She has been on the Waldenbooks bestselling list for romance and won many industry awards. She is a popular speaker at writing organizations and local community functions and has taught creative writing at the University of New Orleans Metropolitan College.

She currently resides in a small community forty miles north of Houston, Texas, with her husband. Though she still has many family and emotional ties to Louisiana, she loves living in the Lone Star state. You may write Joanna at P.O. Box 265, Montgomery, Texas 77356.

Books by Joanna Wayne

HARLEQUIN INTRIGUE
795—A FATHER'S DUTY
867—SECURITY MEASURES
888—THE AMULET
942—A CLANDESTINE AFFAIR
955—MAVERICK CHRISTMAS
975—24/7
1001—24 KARAT AMMUNITION*
1019—TEXAS GUN SMOKE*
1041—POINT BLANK PROTECTOR*
1065—LOADED*

*Four Brothers of Colts Run Cross

CAST OF CHARACTERS

Matt Collingsworth—Second oldest of the Collingsworth brothers. Ranching is all he needs, until Shelly Lane turns his world upside down.

Shelly Lane—CIA operator. The last thing she needs is to fall for someone she's investigating.

Langston Collingsworth—The oldest of the Collingsworth brothers and the president of Collingsworth Oil.

Bart and Zach Collingsworth—Matt's other two brothers.

Lenora Collingsworth—Matt's mother and the CEO of Collingsworth Enterprises.

Becky and Jaime Collingsworth—Matt's sisters.

David and Derrick Collingsworth—Becky's twin sons.

Jeremiah Collingsworth—Matt's grandfather and Shelly's physical therapy patient.

Juanita—Beloved family cook.

Ben Roberts—CIA mole inside Collingsworth Oil.

Melvin Rogers—Langston's right-hand man at Collingsworth Oil and family friend.

Billy Mack—Neighboring rancher.

Angelique Dubois—Famed Houston artist.

Brady Owens—Shelly's supervisor.

Leland Adams—Cowboy who shows up at the big house with Jaime.

Frankie Dawson—Known for his expertise with explosives.

Chapter One

Shelly Lane walked into the Country Café at one-forty on a Friday afternoon in the middle of June, following on the heels of Matt Collingsworth. Smells of fried chicken, cinnamon and fresh-brewed coffee greeted her. It looked like the sort of place you should seat yourself, but a short, plump woman with a knot of graying curls on top of her head was smiling and sashaying toward her.

"Hi, there," the lady said, her charming Texas drawl pulling her words into extra syllables. "You can just sit anywhere, and Jill will be around to take your order in a jiffy."

"Thanks." Shelly glanced around and noted that she was the only one eating alone. Most of the customers were family groups, though there were a few tables with just lone cowboy types. Several looked her way. Most grinned and nodded. A few waved. Colts Run Cross was a very friendly town.

Shelly located Matt—he'd joined a group of men and one super-cute young lady at a table near a window—then chose a spot where she could observe him without making it too obvious. Actually, she didn't mind him seeing her now that she was about to make contact with his mother.

The chair wobbled a bit as she slid it closer to the square

wooden table covered in a blue plaid cloth. A simple vase holding two silk daisies sat in the middle, flanked by inexpensive salt and pepper shakers and a bottle of catsup.

Her attention returned to Matt. He was far more handsome in person than in the likenesses she'd studied of him. His hair was short, dark brown and only slightly rumpled by the Western hat he'd been wearing before entering the restaurant. His jeans were worn, but clean, and though she couldn't see it now, she knew from stealthily following him about town that they showed off his lean, hard frame to perfection.

He glanced her way and smiled. A treacherous skip of her heart forced her to take a deep breath and regroup. Even the slightest attraction on her part could compromise her mission.

Jill stopped at Shelly's elbow. "The special today is fried chicken, mashed potatoes, gravy and pinto beans. That comes with corn bread or biscuits and a dish of peach cobbler and ice cream for dessert. Or you can order off the lunch menu. It's on the back."

The waitress turned the menu over and tapped the offerings with her index finger. "What would you like to drink?"

"Just tea, please, with lemon."

"Sure thing."

Jill stopped off at Matt's table, flirting shamelessly with him and his cohorts. Not that Shelly blamed her. They all had that sexy cowboy mystique about them. It was even more potent than Shelly had expected, but she knew that Matt Collingsworth was no simple cowboy. Nor was he your everyday Texas rancher.

Not only did his family own the second-largest spread in Texas, but they were sole owners of Collingsworth Enterprises, which encompassed the operations of Jack's Bluff Ranch as well as Collingsworth Oil and its related subsidiaries. Which meant they had ties to some of the most high-ranking businessmen and politicians in this country and in other key parts of the world.

The waitress arrived with the tea and Shelly ordered a grilled chicken salad, which arrived in short order. She lingered over her food, finally leaving though Matt was still engaged in a very animated conversation with the others at his table.

The sun was blinding when she stepped out the door of the small café. She fished in her handbag for her sunglasses and put them on as she crossed the street to her dark blue, nondescript sedan. She was opening the door when she spotted a black car rounding the corner, speeding toward her.

Sunlight glinted off the barrel of a revolver as it slid through the open window. Her instincts and training kicked in at the speed of light. She searched the empty streets for someone to warn, then crouched behind the car door as the sound of gunfire and bullets pinging against metal shattered the quiet afternoon.

Even if she'd had time to retrieve her weapon from the car, she wouldn't have had time to fire back. The car had roared past and she could hear the footsteps and voices of people rushing from the nearby shops, before she realized she'd been hit by a ricocheting bullet.

The keys slipped through her fingers and it felt as if a dozen wasps had all found the same spot on the back of her upper arm. Blood soaked the sleeve of her blouse. She stared; the incredulity of the situation made the facts difficult to register. This couldn't have happened. She was CIA and deep undercover. Not even her own mother knew she was in Texas.

"She's been shot," a female yelled.

But when Shelly looked up, she was staring right into the dark, piercing eyes of Matt Collingsworth. Trouble had never been more ominous—or looked so good.

Chapter Two

My name is Shelly Lane. I'm a physical therapist who's just arrived in Colts Run Cross and has no idea why anyone would be shooting at me.

Shelly worked to keep the lies firmly implanted in her mind as she fought to overcome the effects of pain and unexpected vulnerability.

"Some fool fired at me from a passing car and I think a bullet ricocheted into my arm," she said, as Matt crouched down beside her.

"Is that the only place you were hit?"

"I think so."

"You're damn lucky. Your car wasn't so fortunate."

She only nodded, wondering if he was as innocent in all this as he seemed. Her experience told her to doubt him. Her instincts said differently.

"Hope this isn't your favorite blouse," Matt said, wielding a pocketknife and staring at the bloodied mess.

"No, cut away. Not the arm—just the sleeve."

"Picky, are you?" He cut away the fabric and then helped her to the sidewalk where someone had brought out a chair for her to sit on.

"The ambulance is on the way," a bystander announced.

"Who shot her?" someone else yelled.

"Some guy in a black Ford. Skidded around the corner. He's long gone now."

"Son of a bitch!"

"Probably stings like hell," Matt said, shifting so that he could get a better look. "The bullet tore into the flesh of your arm, but there are no exposed bones. A few stitches should put you back together."

He applied pressure to slow the bleeding as she dealt with the bizarre irony of having him come to her rescue. His touch was strangely heady—probably from the rush of adrenaline and the loss of blood. Still, his take-charge attitude was impressive. It was easy to understand why the ranch he comanaged with his bother Bart was so successful.

But then, organizational skills and money were exactly what was making the Collingsworths' ties to terrorists so difficult to trace. She could not let down her guard for a second.

"Who shot at you?" Matt asked.

"I have no idea."

"Do you have that many enemies?"

"I don't have any that I know of. All I know is the car came from nowhere and someone started shooting at me."

"Are you saying this was just a random drive-by?" There was no mistaking the suspicion in his voice.

She tried to move her arm so that she could see the wound.

"Probably best to keep it still," Matt said. "The ambulance will be here soon."

"I don't need an ambulance."

"Maybe not, but you have to go to the emergency room and that's as good a way as any to get there."

"Are you a doctor?"

"Nope, just a rancher. Name's Matt Collingsworth."

"Of Jack's Bluff Ranch?" She hoped there was ample surprise in her pain-laced tone.

"That's right. Have we met?"

"No, I've only been in Colts Run Cross a few days but I have an appointment with Lenora Collingsworth tomorrow at the ranch."

His eyebrows arched.

"I'm the physical therapist she hired for her father-in-law." That much was true. She'd been a physical therapist, before going back to school for a degree in criminal psychology and going to work for the CIA. Her PT background was the only reason she'd drawn this kind of major assignment so early in her career.

"Bum luck to show up in town for a new job and get shot before you even get started," Matt said.

"Do you have many drive-by shootings around here?"

"Never. This makes no sense at all."

And she could tell from his tone and expression that he liked things to make sense. She suspected he also liked being in control. He'd certainly taken over here quickly enough.

"I'll let Mom know not to expect you tomorrow—if ever. I can see how a welcome like this might convince you to turn around and go back home."

Nothing would make her willingly leave before the investigation was completed, but her supervisor was not going to like this development. If the shooting wasn't a random act of violence, then someone had to know who she was and why she was here. In that case, she'd be jerked off the assignment before she even made it to Jack's Bluff Ranch.

A siren sounded and a sheriff's squad car pulled up. A couple of uniformed lawmen jumped out, and the bystanders who had gathered around her all started talking at once.

"A bullet hit the car and…"

"No one saw the shooter, but he was in a sedan…"

"Okay, let's try to talk one at a time," one of the lawmen said. "Did anyone get the license plate number?"

"The car was a black, late-model Ford Fusion, but there was no license plate," Matt said.

"Did you see the whole thing?"

"No, I was inside the café when the shots were fired, but I raced to the window in time to get a good look at the back of the vehicle before it rounded the corner and disappeared from sight."

The lawman put up his hand to signal for quiet. "Did anyone get a look at the shooter?"

"I came running out of Flora's Antique shop when I heard the shots," an overly plump woman with heaving bosoms offered. "All I got was a glimpse of the back of the car."

The others shared similar accounts.

The lawman doing all the talking turned to Shelly. "Did you get a good look at him?"

"No. The second I saw the gun, I ducked out of the way." Which meant there were no eyewitnesses, just as the brazen shooter had no doubt intended.

"Could be some kind of gang-related initiation," one of the young cowboys who'd been sitting with Matt in the café said. "Same thing happened in New Orleans when I was there a few months back helping rebuild a church lost to Katrina."

"Well, hells bells, Charlie. This ain't New Orleans."

The ambulance arrived, and two paramedics jumped out and ran toward her. One started tending the wound that was now only oozing blood. The other commenced with a series of routine questions about the injury and about any allergies she had.

"Let's just hold on here a minute," the lawman-in-charge

interrupted. "I need the victim to answer a couple of questions before you go rushing her to the hospital, seeing as how she's not in dire need of emergency medical care."

He introduced himself as Sheriff Ed Guerra, and she told him her name.

"So, Miss Lane, do you know why anyone would be taking pot shots at you?"

"Absolutely not. I don't know anyone in Colts Run Cross except the people I've met over the last four days. They were all very friendly."

"So you just moved here?"

"I've been staying at the motel on the highway, but I came here to work for the Collingsworths. I'm a physical therapist."

The sheriff and Matt exchanged glances.

"She's supposed to work with Jeremiah," Matt said.

The sheriff nodded and nudged his cowboy hat back a bit farther. "Where are you from?"

"Atlanta."

"That's a long commute."

"I needed a change of scenery and I've always wanted to visit Texas."

"How did you hear about a job at Jack's Bluff Ranch?"

"I found the *Houston Chronicle* classifieds online and saw the Collingsworths' ad."

He nodded and scratched his clean-shaven chin. "Guess that makes sense. The rest of my questions can wait until you get that arm cleaned and stitched." He nodded to the medics. "She's all yours."

She let them load her into the ambulance. Her arm still hurt, but her biggest problem right now was finding out who had shot at her and why—before her supervisor determined she wasn't the person for this assignment.

If he found out that she'd let Matt Collingsworth get to her for even a second, he'd pull her anyway. But he needn't worry. She was focused now and would make sure that Matt's masculine sexuality and piercing eyes did not affect her again.

Her mission was to infiltrate the family and ferret out the full truth, an accomplishment that would likely destroy the Collingsworth empire and send at least some of the family members to prison for the rest of their lives.

She'd do the legwork. A judge and jury would decide the rest.

"THE PATIENT'S AWAKE NOW, Lenora. You can go in, but don't expect her to be too talkative. That pain medication is making her drowsy."

"I just want to say hello and make sure she doesn't need anything." Lenora knocked and then entered the hospital room where her would-be new employee lay beneath a pale blue blanket with an IV attached to her right arm. Her eyes were watchful as Lenora stepped to the side of the bed.

"I'm Lenora Collingsworth."

Shelly smiled and tried to push up on her elbows, giving up on the idea quickly and dropping back to the pillow. "It's nice to finally meet you, though this isn't exactly how I'd pictured the moment."

She had a nice smile and a sense of humor. She was attractive, too, with short brown hair specked with gold, and half bangs that set off her beautiful gold-green eyes.

Lenora placed her hand on the bed rail. "I can't believe this happened after I assured you that you were coming to a safe area. But in all honesty, I don't remember a single case of a random, drive-by shooting in Colts Run Cross. In parts of Houston, yes. But never in our community."

"It wasn't your fault," Shelly said. "In hindsight, I should have come straight to the ranch, but it's my first visit to Texas and I wanted to do a bit of sightseeing before I began work."

"Well, at least you got to do that. I don't want to tire you, but I wanted to let you know how sorry I am and to make certain you have everything you need."

"I appreciate that, but I don't plan to be in this bed long. The doctor stitched me back together and is giving me antibiotics and some pain medication. He says I'll be good as new soon. I'll likely leave the hospital tomorrow."

"Where will you go?"

"Back to the motel, I guess. I can't expect you to provide room and board until this arm heals and I can start work."

"Nonsense," Lenora said, relieved that Shelly wasn't planning to renege on their agreement. "You can have all the time you need to heal at the ranch. It will give you a chance to get to know Jeremiah before you start treating him. As I told you on the phone, he's a bit cantankerous since the stroke. Well, more than a bit at times, but he can be loveable when he wants to be."

"That would be great—if you're sure I won't be imposing."

"Not at all. I'll check with the hospital in the morning," Lenora said. "If the doctor releases you, I'll either pick you up myself or have someone else in the family do it, depending on their schedules. Whoever drives you to the ranch can stop off at the motel for your luggage. In the meantime, I'll have the housekeeper get your room ready."

"I have my own car, still parked on the street in front of the café."

"Matt had it towed to Hank Tanner's body shop once the sheriff and his men had finished examining it. Hank will keep it there until you have a chance to look at it and decide what you want done. No strings attached."

"So the vehicle was examined?"

"Yes, of course, dear. Ed Guerra and his department are very efficient. And don't worry about the cost of the bodywork on your vehicle. I'll cover whatever your insurance doesn't. It's the least I can do."

"I couldn't ask you to do that."

"I insist."

"Thanks. That's a very generous offer, but I'm sure the insurance will handle it. I guess all I have to do now is give my arm a little time to heal. I can't wait to actually get started."

"Just hold on to that attitude once you meet Jeremiah."

"I promise."

Lenora had a feeling that this was going to work out perfectly in spite of the troublesome start. The shooting still worried her, but she'd checked Shelly's references thoroughly. There was no reason to think this was any more than a random shooting perpetrated by some hoodlum who'd been high on drugs. It was the sheriff's job to take care of that.

The positive news was that a smart, attractive woman who was unfazed by gunfire could surely handle Jeremiah. She might even be able to stir a little romantic excitement in Matt. If any man needed a woman, it was him—not that he'd ever admit it.

Lenora found herself humming as she left the hospital. This just might turn into a very memorable summer. In fact, she was counting on it.

"SHOT AT FROM A PASSING CAR right on Main Street?" Incredulity colored Jaime's tone and lit up her eyes. "And just when I was thinking of moving into Houston to add a little excitement to my ho-hum life."

"It's not funny," Lenora said. "She could have been killed."

"Sorry, Mom. I didn't mean it that way. But you have to admit it's unusual. There has to be more to the story than that."

"Things like this happen in big cities all the time," Lenora said. "It was inevitable it would make its way out here eventually. There's no reason to believe Shelly did anything to provoke the attempt on her life."

Matt had known the topic of the shooting would come up sooner or later. In fact, he was surprised they'd made it all the way through dinner before Lenora had approached the subject.

They'd gathered on the huge screened back porch, and since it was Friday, several extended family members were still sitting around catching up on the week's happenings.

The shooting had been front and center on Matt's mind all afternoon, and the more he thought about it, the more he was convinced that the best news for them would be if Shelly Lane decided to pack her bags and move right back to Atlanta. She might be totally innocent in all of this, but the odds were that she wasn't.

"Tell me more about this woman," Langston said, after Lenora had given them the few details they knew about the gunfire incident. Langston was the oldest, the head honcho of Collingsworth Oil. He had a cabin at the ranch, but lived in Houston during the week with his pregnant wife Trish and teenage daughter Gina.

"Shelly seems really nice," Lenora said. "And mature for her age. A lot of young women would have panicked and been ready to clear out of town as fast as they could. She only wants to heal and start working with Jeremiah."

"How old is she?" Trish asked.

"Twenty-nine," Lenora said. "But she's experienced and a very competent physical therapist. I checked her credentials thoroughly before hiring her."

"Twenty-nine. Very interesting. And single, I'm guessing, since she's moving in with us." Jaime added. "And Matt's thirty-three. How convenient, not that Mom would ever play matchmaker." That brought a few laughs.

Matt groaned. His mother had managed to manipulate him into situations with half the single women in Colts Run Cross over the last few months. He hadn't taken the bait then and he wouldn't be biting this time, either, certainly not with a city girl out here for a change of scenery.

"This isn't about Matt," Lenora said. "It's about Jeremiah."

His grandfather picked that moment to join them on the porch. He propped his cane against the old wicker couch and dropped to the cushioned seat. "What about me?"

"I've hired a physical therapist," Lenora said. "She's from Georgia, but she's going to live with us and help you regain your balance and strength."

He sputtered and muttered a few curses under his breath. "If I wanted to be manhandled by a woman, I'd have remarried."

Trish walked over and sat down by Jeremiah. She had a way with the old codger, but then she pretty much had a way with everyone.

"Having a live-in therapist seems the perfect solution to me," Trish said. "You never want to go to your appointments. This way you won't have to."

"I don't go to therapy because the sessions don't do a dad-gummed bit of good. If they did, I wouldn't be hobbling around here like some useless old man, now would I?"

"You limp," Trish admitted. "But you could never be useless."

I've hired Shelly Lane," Lenora said. "If you want to get rid of that cane, you'll cooperate with her. If you're too hard-headed to work with her, then it will be your loss. She's moving in tomorrow." Lenora dusted her hands as if that were the end of the matter, but that didn't mean it was.

"Tomorrow?" Jaime questioned. "I thought this new physical therapist was in the hospital."

Lenora kicked off her black sandals and pulled a foot into the chair with her, settling it under her full black skirt. "If not tomorrow, then the next day. She's coming here to recuperate."

"Are you sure that's a good idea?" Langston questioned.

"Why wouldn't it be? She doesn't have anywhere else to go," Lenora said. "Besides, it will give her a chance to get to know Jeremiah before she starts working with him."

"Yeah, like that's an advantage," Jaime mocked.

Matt's muscles tightened. "I know you mean well, Mom, but you can't just move her onto the ranch until we have more facts about today's attack."

"What's to know?" Lenora asked. "She was just crossing the street and someone started firing at her. You were the one who told me what happened, Matt. That's why I went to the hospital to check on her."

"That's the way it looked," Matt said, "and the way Shelly told it, but at this point there's no way to know she's leveling with us. The shooter could be someone she knows."

Jeremiah swung his cane in the air, banging it into the leg of a table and sending a half-empty glass of iced tea into a wobbling dance that fortunately ended without the glass hitting the floor. "Don't know what this world's coming to, but if some sick bastard's trying to kill her, you ought to already have her out here. Can't expect a woman to take care of herself."

"Right," Jaime said, mocking him. "What would we ever do without a man to take care of us?"

"Let's get back to Shelly Lane," Langston said. "She's probably as innocent in all this as she claims, but to be on the safe side, I'd like to have Clay Markham investigate her before we move her onto Jack's Bluff. He's as competent a private detective as you'll find anywhere in Texas, and Collingsworth Oil has him on retainer."

"And I say we get Aidan Jefferies to run a police background check on her as well," Matt said. "If they both clear her, then Mom can move her in with no worries." Aidan was one of Langston's closest friends and a Houston homicide detective.

"How long are we talking about for these investigations?" Lenora asked.

"A few days at most," Langston assured her. "Actually, they'll probably know by tomorrow night if she's had any other attempts on her life or reported any type of threats. They'll definitely know if she has a police record of any kind."

"I guess I can live with that," Lenora said, "though I hate to tell her that I'm going back on my offer to move her out here tomorrow. And I don't like the idea of her going back to that motel all alone."

"Have the doctor keep her in the hospital," Matt said. "I don't know why he'd object to that, as long as we pick up the tab."

"I suppose that's an option," Lenora said. "And tomorrow's probably not the best day to have her out here, anyway, what with children from the Turnaround Program coming out for the day."

Matt groaned. "That's tomorrow?"

"Yes, and you promised to help with the horse riding,"

Lenora said, smoothing her short graying hair. "I'll give Shelly's doctor a call, but I guess I should go back into town tonight and break the news to Shelly in person."

"I'll do it," Matt said, suddenly uneasy with his mother becoming too involved with Shelly before they had an official report.

"Okay, but don't tell her the delay is because we're having her investigated. Just say I'm getting her room ready so that everything will be perfect when she arrives."

Matt shrugged. "Sorry, Mom, I'm not into sugarcoating."

"Just be nice," Lenora said. "Miss Lane's welcome to Texas has already been traumatic enough."

"I'm always nice."

"Compared to what?" Jaime asked. "A striking rattlesnake?"

"Just because I'm not a pushover for a smile and a pretty face doesn't mean I'm unsociable."

"Pretty, huh?" Jaime smiled tauntingly. "This story just keeps getting better. But I'll have to hear the rest tomorrow. I've got a date with Tommy Stevens tonight, and he should be here to pick me up any minute."

"When did you start dating him?" Trish asked. "I thought you were back with Garth."

"Not anymore. All he thinks about is running off to some new rodeo competition. Like at twenty-five, don't you think he'd have better things to do than try to stay on a stupid bull?"

Matt would have thought the guy had better things to do than date Jaime. She was as fickle as a mare at breeding time. But all she had to do was crook her finger and Garth—and half the male population of south Texas—came running. He hoped someone would shoot him if he ever got that crazy about any woman.

His cell phone rang. He checked the caller ID: sheriff's

office. He walked to the kitchen to take the call. Ten to one this had to do with Shelly Lane, and the odds were even better that it was not good news.

Chapter Three

"What's up, Ed?" Matt asked as soon as the sheriff identified himself.

"I just talked to Emile Henley up at the Shell Station on the highway west of town. He said a stranger in a black Ford Fusion stopped for gas at his place about an hour before today's shooting."

"That's interesting. Did he think the man might have been drunk or high on something?"

"Nope, just buck-snorting arrogant according to Emile. He said he tried to make small talk when the guy came inside for cigarettes, but the man just made some comment about Colts Run Cross being a hick town and stomped away."

"Did he notice if the car had a license plate on it at the time?"

"Said he didn't notice."

"But he likely would have if the plate had been missing. The culprit probably removed it just before opening fire on Shelly Lane."

"That's what I'm thinking as well. I'd be careful if I was you about moving her onto the ranch. She seems nice enough, but truth is she might be mixed up in most anything."

"I'm in solid agreement. If it were up to me, I'd write out

a check for her time and expenses and say adios, but Mom is championing her case—as if she were the only qualified PT north of the border."

"I hear you, and your mother can be a stubborn woman at times. Can you call Miss Lane to the phone?"

"I'd have to yell awful loud. I'm out at the ranch."

"Isn't she there with you?"

"No, why would you think that?"

"I stopped by the hospital a few minutes ago to question her and the nurse said she checked herself out and told them she would be spending the night at Jack's Bluff Ranch. I figured Lenora had picked her up."

"No, Mom's been here all evening. So have I. Shelly Lane is definitely not here."

"This case is getting weirder by the minute."

"Is there something more about her past?"

"Not a lot. I ran her through the system. Everything checks out. No warrants out for her arrest. No rap sheet. Not even an outstanding parking ticket."

"So you're thinking this might have actually been a case of random violence?"

"Could be. There's been a rash of them in southeast Houston of late. We're less than an hour and a half out of the city so it's reasonable that some of the hoods down there might have connections up here. But then there was the gun."

"Are you saying you found the weapon?"

"Not the perp's, but when we were checking Miss Lane's vehicle for ballistic evidence, I found a loaded Smith & Wesson .45 in her busted-up glove compartment. It might mean nothing. Lots of women traveling alone carry high-powered pistols these days."

"But it could mean she was afraid of someone," Matt said, "someone who followed her to Texas."

"Exactly."

As far as Matt was concerned, this was beginning to look more and more like the pretty little PT had better reasons than a need for change of scenery for taking a job so far from home. And now she'd lied about where she'd be tonight.

But no matter what she'd told the nurse at the hospital, it was a sure thing she wouldn't be spending tonight, or any other night, at Jake's Bluff Ranch until he got to the bottom of this.

FORTUNATELY FOR SHELLY, Hank Tanner's Garage and Body Shop was on Birch, a quiet side street of mostly closed family-owned businesses less than a mile from the hospital. It should have been an easy twilight walk except that the temperature was still in the eighties and the humidity seemed higher still.

Perspiration wet her underarms and dripped into her eyes. Worse, her arm had stated to throb. Wiping her face with a tissue from her pocket, she crossed the street and turned the corner, thankful when she spotted the sign for the garage in the next block. Her spirits lifted more when she saw her car parked at the side of the old clapboard building.

Hopefully her weapon was still in place. The sheriff would have surely checked the damaged vehicle for ballistics evidence, but he'd have had no reason to check her locked glove compartment. But then he probably had the keys. She didn't remember giving them to anyone, but either she had or she'd dropped them when she got shot.

Stepping over a crack in the sidewalk, she cut across the corner of the parking lot, walked around the rear of an old pickup truck and got her first good look at the extent of the damage to her vehicle.

The whole side of the car was riddled with bullet holes.

She hadn't gotten a good look at the weapon, but judging from the size and number of holes, it must have been a large automatic. Her nerves grew edgy as it hit her how close she'd come to getting killed.

Attacked in broad daylight on the main street of Colts Run Cross. She could see why that might rouse both the sheriff's and Matt Collingsworth's suspicions, but what else could it be except random violence?

The only people with reason not to want her here were the Collingsworths, and it was almost inconceivable that they could have learned her identity this quickly. And even if they had, a careless, open attack like this wasn't their style.

She let her fingers slide over the damage, then walked to the passenger-side door, opened it and climbed inside. The vehicle wasn't locked, but even if it had been, entry would have been easy enough with two windows shot out.

Her spirits plunged at the first glimpse inside the glove compartment. The contents—including her weapon—were missing.

There was the possibility that Hank Tanner had her belongings inside for safekeeping, but more likely the sheriff had confiscated them. No problem there. The car and gun registrations would check out.

Still, it was amazing how vulnerable she felt without her weapon, despite the fact that she hadn't carried it on her body since arriving in Colts Run Cross. It didn't fit the PT persona and chancing someone noticing that she was carrying a weapon would constitute an unnecessary risk when there was no reason to think she was in any kind of danger.

Her cell phone vibrated—not her regular phone but the CIA one, disguised as a compact. It was her signal to call in at her earliest convenience unless she was free to take the call. She wished she could ignore it, because it was likely her supervisor and she wasn't sure she was ready to handle Brady Owens just yet. She took a deep breath and leaned against the car.

"Shelly Lane," she said, identifying herself.

"I got the word you've been shot," Brady said, without bothering with a greeting. "Are you okay?"

"Yeah, or I will be in a few days. It was only a flesh wound. Left arm. Random violence. Nothing to worry about—really."

"Any complication is reason for worry. Where are you?"

"At Hank Tanner's Garage, standing by my vehicle."

"Who's with you?"

"I'm alone. I wouldn't have answered otherwise."

"I'm just checking."

To see if the accident had somehow addled her brain and made her a risk. The Collingsworth case was Brady's baby and he'd made it clear that he wasn't comfortable with her lack of experience. She was certain he'd be even less thrilled with her now.

"I'm totally aware of the seriousness of this case, sir, but things are under control. What I meant is there's no reason the assignment shouldn't still be a go."

"That will be my decision. I haven't made it yet."

"Yes, sir."

"Have there been any new developments since you called in the report?"

"Nothing except that I've left the hospital."

"Were you released?"

"No, sir, but the wound is too insignificant to require hospitalization. I'll go back in tomorrow to have it checked."

"See that you do that. Is there anything else I should know?"

"My weapon was locked in the glove compartment of my

car at the time of the shooting incident. It's missing. I assume either the mechanic took it for safekeeping or the sheriff has it. Either way, I'm sure I'll get it back."

"Just be sure to explain it away convincingly. Do you think there is any chance the Collingsworths were behind the attack?"

"I'm all but certain they weren't. Matt Collingsworth was inside the restaurant when it occurred and was the first to come to my rescue."

"So I heard. That doesn't mean he couldn't have ordered a hit. With his money, hired guns are easy to come by."

"But we have no evidence that any of the Collingsworths have ever used a paid assassin," Shelly countered. "And Lenora Collingsworth visited me at the hospital. She seemed extremely apologetic about the shooting incident and has asked me to move to the ranch tomorrow. That would be the last thing she'd do if she knew I was with the CIA."

"It would seem that way, unless you're walking into a trap."

"They're not going to shoot me in cold blood," Shelly said. "They use money and influence—not guns—to get what they want." Shelly knew that Brady would have a difficult time denying that.

Besides, she was his best chance—maybe his only chance—to get an agent inside the family circle, and they needed that edge to push things off dead center.

They'd had a mole inside Collingsworth Oil for months. Ben Hartmann was an experienced agent and talented computer hacker, but as yet he hadn't acquired the proof to seal the case. No proof that the Collingsworths were GAS, Ben's term for suspects once they had indisputable evidence that they were *guilty as sin*.

"We've spent weeks setting this up," she argued. "Unless

there's a serious leak in our department, no one could possibly have found out why I'm really here. It would be a major setback if we called this off just because some two-bit hood with a point to prove to his fellow gang members shot up my car."

"The random violence angle is a huge assumption, Shelly. You know what I think about assumptions."

"Yes, sir." But he also knew there was always a gamble in this type of operation.

"I'd like to hear your firsthand, no-spin account of today's shooting incident."

She filled him in on the details, leaving nothing out—except for her ridiculous and very momentary attraction to Matt Collingsworth. He listened without questions until she'd finished.

Then the silence on the line seemed thick with apprehension. She knew he was rethinking everything, especially her inexperience. She didn't breathe easy until she heard the muffled clicking of his tongue against the roof of his mouth, a clear signal that he was giving in. All the agents recognized the telltale habit.

"Proceed as planned, while I have this checked into, Shelly. But watch your back and stay on high alert. Never underestimate a Collingsworth."

"That's a given."

Once the connection was broken, she stepped outside the car and looked around. It was almost completely dark now and a sliver of moon hung just over the top of a cluster of sweet gum trees on the opposite side of the street.

There were a couple of other businesses on the block—a machine shop and a tree-trimming business. Both were closed with no sign of life around the buildings, except a black cat, crouched near a trash bin, cautiously watching Shelly.

A welcome gust of wind caught an empty bag and blew it across the parking lot depositing it under Shelly's banged-up vehicle. Thankfully it was not actually her car, but one the agency had purchased specifically for this assignment.

A pickup truck turned the corner onto Birch, the beam from its headlights fanning her for an instant before returning to the street. The driver slowed, and in spite of her mental reassurances of safety, her nerves skittered nervously.

It's a small town, she told herself as the driver pulled into the parking lot a few feet away. He was probably just curious why a woman would be out here all alone. Still, she'd feel a lot safer with her weapon in hand. Today's close call had been an excellent reminder that she wasn't invincible.

The car stopped, and she got her first good luck at the driver. Her muscles clenched. This wasn't a curious passerby.

He was here to find her.

Chapter Four

Matt slid from behind the wheel and stood by the side of his truck, his gaze fixed on Shelly. Her face and eyes were shadowed, her features blurred in the early-evening darkness. She looked pale, but her shoulders were squared and her mouth was set in hard lines as if she was determined not to let the situation get the better of her.

An unexpected protective urge surged inside him as his focus moved to her bandaged arm and then to the bullet-battered car.

"We've got to stop meeting like this," she quipped, but her attempt at humor lost its effect to the eerie screech of an owl hidden in the branches of a nearby tree.

Matt looked around, expecting to see Hank standing nearby. He didn't. The place was completely deserted except for Shelly.

"What are you doing here after hours?" he asked.

Shelly brushed her bangs to one side and propped her right hand on her hip almost defiantly. "I could ask you the same thing."

"I was looking for you," he admitted. "I tried your motel. When you weren't there, I drove here to see if Hank had heard from you."

"How did you know I'd left the hospital?"

"The sheriff called me. Apparently you told the nursing staff you were going to Jack's Bluff tonight."

She shrugged and looked backed to the car as he stepped closer. "I didn't exactly tell them that. They just surmised it and I didn't set them straight. It seemed the easiest way to walk out of the hospital without causing a major ruckus."

"Why not just wait until the doctor released you?"

"I hate hospitals and I didn't see any point in running up a big hospital bill when I didn't need to be there in the first place."

Matt scanned the quiet parking lot. "How did you get here?"

"I walked. It's not that far." She slapped at a mosquito that was buzzing around her ear. "I'm fine, Matt. And I don't hold your family responsible for any of this, if that's what you're worried about."

"I'm not worried at all." Unfortunately, that wasn't exactly true. Pretty much everything about Shelly Lane worried him—and puzzled him—especially the fact that she was standing on a deserted street alone at night after being shot at just hours ago.

He didn't trust this whole situation, wasn't at all convinced that Shelly didn't know who'd tried to kill her. Yet if she did, that would give her all the more reason not to put herself at risk like this.

He stepped between her and the car. "Are you in some kind of trouble, Shelly?"

"No. Why would you ask that? You were there when some crackpot roared in from nowhere and used my car for target practice."

"The other possibility is that he'd come to town looking for you."

"Don't be ridiculous. I don't even know anyone around this part of the country."

"Maybe someone followed you from Atlanta. Maybe a jealous boyfriend? A jilted lover?"

"The last boyfriend is engaged to be married to a fashion model. He forgot me at the first sight of my replacement—who I introduced him to, no less."

Matt doubted that any man had found Shelly that easy to forget, but he wasn't going there now. He pressed a hand on the top of the car and leaned into it. "Do you always carry a loaded gun in your glove compartment?"

She turned to look at his truck and the shotgun riding the rack behind his seat. "Obviously there's no local law against carrying weapons in a vehicle."

"Touché."

"Actually, one of my friends insisted I buy it before leaving Atlanta. She kept stressing how it wasn't safe for a woman to drive so far by herself, said I might have car trouble and get stranded in a dangerous area. Who knew the danger would be in Colts Run Cross?"

Which is what made this so difficult to buy into. He watched as the breeze teased her bangs, blowing wispy strands of hair about her forehead.

"I'm shaken, Matt. I won't deny it. My first instinct was to go running back to Atlanta. But running from random violence is like trying to get out of the path of a tornado. It can strike anywhere."

"But both are more likely in some places than others." The owl screeched again and mosquitoes were starting to treat the back of his neck like a buffet. Whatever was going on with Shelly Lane, he was pretty sure he wasn't going to get to the bottom of it tonight.

Matt rocked back on the heels of his boots. "No point in

hanging around out here," he said. "I can give you a ride back to your motel."

"Thanks."

And on the way he'd tell her that her plan to move to the ranch tomorrow had been put on hold.

They walked back to his truck in silence and he opened the door for her. He circled the vehicle, climbed behind the wheel, turned the key in the ignition and gunned the engine. The beams of his headlights illuminated the damaged side of Shelly's car as he backed from the lot.

His hands tightened on the wheel as the reality of the situation settled into a grim knot in his stomach. If the attack on her was personal, the guy wouldn't just give up because the first try didn't work. The shooter might even be a hired hit man biding his time until he could get to her again. Maybe waiting for dark, when she was alone in a motel at the edge of town.

A spray of gravel shot from the back wheels of his pickup truck as he sped away from Hank's. He couldn't take her to the ranch when no one knew for certain she was on the up and up. But he couldn't just dump her to fend for herself if she was in real danger.

So where did that leave him?

SHELLY SAT UP STRAIGHTER, staring at the neon sign identifying the rambling wooden roadhouse whose parking lot they'd just pulled into as Cutter's Bar and Grill.

"Why are you stopping here?"

"I could use a cup of coffee," Matt said.

"I don't drink coffee this late," she said.

"Then how about a beer?"

"I can't drink alcohol. I'm still feeling the effects of the pain medication they gave me at the hospital. Besides I'm not dressed for going out."

That wasn't exactly a valid argument since she had on the same jeans she'd had on at lunch today. Topping them was the crimson cami she'd had on under the bloodied blouse that Matt had cut the sleeves out of. There was a blood stain on it, but it so closely matched the color of the shirt, it looked more like fabric shading. Her attire would likely be the same as half the women in the bar.

"You look fine," Matt said, "and I could really use the coffee."

She hesitated, then pulled down the visor and checked her reflection in the small lighted mirror. "I at least have to put on some lipstick," she said, already reaching in her handbag for a tube. She'd have never gone out in D.C. looking like this, but she wasn't in the nation's capital and this wasn't a date. It was her job. This might be the perfect opportunity to start winning Matt's confidence.

Matt took her arm as they crossed the parking lot and walked through the open doorway. Shelly took in the sights and the atmosphere.

Cute cowboys in Western shirts, jeans and boots perched on worn wooden barstools and drank beer from bottles and whiskey and Tequila from shot glasses. Couples filled the dance floor, two-stepping to a slow country ballad.

Matt exchanged waves and greetings with some of the patrons as he led Shelly to the left side of the main room, away from the bar and dance floor. Couples and small groups were enjoying late dinners. Odors of fried onions and peppery spices hung heavy in the air; there was a refreshing absence of stale cigarette smoke and Shelly assumed Cutter's Bar had followed suit with many other Texas restaurants and bars and allowed smoking only outside the building.

Most of the patrons were in their early to mid twenties,

but there were some older customers as well, including a group of six women who looked to be their late fifties.

They seemed to be having the most fun of all, laughing and talking loudly. One of the older women caught Matt's eye and waved him over. The other women at the table seemed equally as delighted to see him as Shelly and Matt maneuvered through the maze of tables and mismatched chairs.

Shelly knew from her research that all the Collingsworths were not only well-liked but respected throughout this part of Texas. Watching Matt, it was easy to see why. He wore his wealth the way she might wear a pair of old jeans. Easy. Comfortably. Free of even the slightest pretension.

"This table looks like solid trouble," Matt said, leaning over to kiss the cheek of the one who'd initially spotted him. "What are you gorgeous hens doing out without the roosters?"

"They're all over in Austin at a cattle auction, so we decided to hit the town."

"Look out, cowboys," Matt said.

"Land sakes, we don't want them," one woman said.

"Right," another agreed. "We just got rid of our own. We're just here to eat someone else's cooking."

"And have company that doesn't moo."

They all laughed again and Matt introduced Shelly to the rancher's wives. She felt an unexpected twinge of guilt that they accepted her so readily when she was here under false pretenses. But how could these women, or anyone else in this town possibly know the traitorous paths that the Collingsworths had followed?

Make that had *allegedly* followed, but the evidence against them was overwhelming—just not indisputable as yet.

Matt spoke and waved to several more people before they finally stopped at a table near the back, where it was only slightly quieter. He held her chair for her, then took the seat opposite hers. She was keenly aware that in a bar full of sexy cowboys, he still stood out.

It wasn't his looks that set him apart, though he certainly held his own in that department. It was his self-confidence, Shelly decided. He was a man who knew who he was and what he was about.

A waitress sashayed over, and true to his word, Matt ordered a black coffee.

"If you're hungry, they have great burgers here," he said. "Good chicken-fried steaks, too."

Shelly had learned quickly that battered and fried steak— as big as the plate and covered in thick cream gravy—was a staple of every restaurant in this part of Texas. She'd tried it, and loved it. Then promptly gave it up before she gained too much weight to fit into the new jeans she'd purchased for this assignment.

"I can bring you a menu," the waitress said. "Kitchen's open until midnight."

"Thanks, but I won't need one. The burger sounds good."

"With cheese, jalapenos, onion rings?"

"Just cheese. And a glass of iced tea, unsweetened."

Shelly wasn't hungry, though she'd barely touched her dinner at the hospital. But picking at food would be less awkward than having nothing to do but stare at Matt, while he bombarded her with questions that she'd be forced to answer with rehearsed lies.

She was certain that's what this coffee date was about. He was obviously suspicious of the day's events and determined to check her out. That convinced her even more that neither he nor his family had any idea who she really was. All she had to do was play this cool and she'd soon be living inside the gates of Jack's Bluff Ranch.

"Don't you drink beer?" she asked when the waitress walked away.

"Occasionally. Mostly I'm a whiskey man, but I had a drink after dinner and I figure that's enough. I have an early day tomorrow"

"It's Saturday."

"Cows don't know that. Besides, I'm helping out with one of Mom's do-gooder events tomorrow."

"What does that entail?"

"This is her Turnaround Project where she brings a group of inner-city preteens out to get a feel for ranch life. They're kids who've been in trouble in school and sometimes with the law. Behaviorally something or other."

"Behaviorally challenged?"

"That's it. Or as Jeremiah says, undisciplined brats. They usually come in with huge chips on their shoulders, but by the time they leave, most are strutting around and grinning like rodeo champs."

"Sounds interesting."

"For the most part." The waitress returned with Matt's coffee and Shelly's tea. "Tell me about you," he said, once the waitress walked away.

"What do you want to know?"

"Guess we should start with the basics."

"Name, rank and serial number?"

"I was thinking more along the line of why a woman from the big city is looking to work in Colts Run Cross?"

"A thirst for adventure, though today's excitement wasn't exactly what I had in mind."

"Were you giving private, live-in care in Atlanta?"

"No, I worked for a rehab center." She told him something about the setting and the work, all verifiable if he checked.

"I take it you're not married," Matt said.

"No. I came close once. It didn't work out. What about you?" she asked, though she knew he was single.

"Never came close."

"That's hard to believe."

"Why?"

He stared at her with his steely gray, almost brooding eyes, and a tingle that felt far too much like anticipation zinged along her nerve endings. This was completely unlike her—and too dangerous and unprofessional for words.

She forced herself to picture Matt with huge warts on his nose and thick bushy eyebrows that jutted out like porcupine quills.

"It's just that most men have either been married or had a close call or two by the time they reach your age," she said, going for an easy nonchalance.

He smiled, and the warts vanished. "I have a few more years before Medicare kicks in."

She blushed in spite of herself. "I didn't mean that the way it came out."

"It's okay. The truth is, I'm not the marrying kind."

"Tell me about Jeremiah," Shelly said, hoping to get the conversation on safer ground. "Your mother indicated he can be a bit difficult at times."

"She said that, did she? Let's just say that dealing with my grandfather on a daily basis will make this afternoon's trouble seem like a bad dream."

She grimaced. "That bad, huh?"

Matt worried the handle of his mug. "Before the stroke, my grandfather was the CEO of Collingsworth Enterprises and went into his Houston office five days a week. The only concession he'd made to aging was that he'd hired a driver a few years back to fight the traffic for him while he read the morning paper and made phone calls.

"Now he refuses to set foot in the building. He claims he's not interested, but we all know that he just doesn't want to go back there and have his former employees see him hobbling around and relying on the cane."

Jeremiah's stroke had caused a few problems for the CIA, as well. As CEO and with a reputation for being a hard-edge and aggressive businessman, he'd been the focus of their initial investigation. They'd suspected that he might be totally responsible for the terrorist funding in exchange for favorable business deals and that the rest of the family might not even be aware of his illegal dealings.

But when he'd suffered the stroke and disappeared from the picture, the illegal and traitorous activities had actually surged, making it obvious that at least one other member of the family was in on the illegal scheme, perhaps even Lenora Collingsworth who'd replaced Jeremiah as CEO.

"So lots of luck with the old codger," Matt said.

"Thanks. I have a feeling I'll need it."

The waitress returned and placed the burger in front of Shelly. The mammoth toasted bun spilled over with leafy green lettuce and thick slices of the bright red, home-grown tomatoes Shelly had gotten used to since arriving in Colts Run Cross.

Not surprisingly, her appetite sprang to life. Halfway through the burger, she let her gaze scan the row of men and women seated at the bar. A tall, lanky man on the end was staring back at her.

He was in his late twenties, she'd guess, with light brown hair that crawled into his shirt collar. No visible tattoos, but his nose had a slight crook to it as if it had been broken and not reset properly. Still, he was cute enough in a rugged sort of way.

When their gazes locked, he tipped his beer in her direction as if they might have met before. He was probably just one of the locals she'd crossed paths with over the past few days. Still, a wary tremble of foreboding slithered up her spine. She couldn't afford to have someone from her distant past show up and recognize her as shy little Ann Clark from Biloxi, Mississippi.

But he'd seemingly forgotten her now and was flirting with a young woman who'd just sidled in beside him at the bar. Shelly pushed the rest of the burger away. "Do you mind if we go now, Matt? My arm is starting to throb a bit."

"No problem." He motioned to the waitress for their check.

"Do you know what time Lenora is picking me up tomorrow?" Shelly asked. "I'd like to be packed and ready to go when she arrives."

Matt propped his elbows on the table and leaned in closer. "I'm afraid there's been a slight change in plans."

Her guard went up. "What kind of change?"

"I'm going to give this to you straight, Shelly. My brothers and I aren't totally convinced you've been on the up and up with us."

Acid trickled and burned along the lining of her stomach. If she handled this wrong, the whole assignment could go up in smoke. "I'm not sure what you're getting at."

"Just that the kind of random violence we saw today has been previously unheard of in Colts Run Cross."

"So you think that he had to be targeting me?"

"That makes more sense."

"Sorry to disappoint you, Matt, but I don't have those kind of enemies. And if I did know who'd shot at me, why on earth would I lie about it?"

"You tell me."

She feigned an indignant expression and straightened her

back and shoulders. "What difference does it make what I say if you think I'm a liar?"

"I'm not saying you're lying. Having you checked out by a private investigator is just a reasonable precaution. It's not personal."

"Really? It sounds extremely personal to me." But it was not a problem for her. *You go for it, Matt Collingsworth. Check all you want. The CIA has me covered.*

"In all likelihood, we're only talking a couple of days here," Matt said. "I'll cover your expenses at the motel or, if you'd prefer, I can drive you into Houston and book you a room in a more luxurious hotel."

Why not? Money was no object for the Collingsworths.

"The motel's fine. I can wait around there until you decide if I pass muster," she said, "as long as it doesn't take too long." She stood to go, grabbing her handbag from the back of her chair and slinging it over her shoulder.

"There is one more thing," Matt said.

"Let me guess. You want me to stay handcuffed to the bed in the motel until you're sure I'm not luring evil into your quaint little Texas town."

He smiled again, a kind of taunting, half smile that tightened her chest. Not attraction, she told herself. She had that totally under control.

"Handcuffs sound interesting," Matt said, "but I was thinking of something a little less dramatic."

"Such as?"

"Until we know why someone tried to kill you today, I don't think you should stay alone."

"Do you have a better idea?"

"Yeah. I'm staying with you."

She couldn't have heard him right. A man like Matt Collingsworth didn't put himself out for a prospective employee whom he suspected might be a blatant liar. But then she wouldn't have expected one of the richest men in Texas to be sitting across from her tonight in a Texas roadhouse, either.

"What did you say?" she asked.

"On the off chance that the guy who shot you today was looking to kill you specifically, you shouldn't be alone tonight."

"And you're planning to serve as my bodyguard?"

"Why not? I've never gone up against a killer before, but I've handled some bulls that were looking to leave my kidneys scattered over the rodeo ring."

"That isn't necessary."

"Actually, it is. Family tradition, the cowboy code and all that. A real man never walks away from a woman in danger, even one with a loaded Smith & Wesson in her possession."

He'd walk away fast enough if he knew she was CIA— here to put him and his family away for life. But he didn't know, and for now, it would apparently be only her and Matt in a slightly shady motel on the edge of town. Breathing the same stale air stirred by the whirring ceiling fan and over-worked air conditioner. Perhaps close enough she'd hear the rustle of sheets when he shifted positions.

She should be thanking her lucky stars for this entrée into the inner sanctum of the world she'd come to infiltrate. But only one word came to mind and it seemed to be shouting inside her head and echoing through every cell of her body.

Help!

Chapter Five

Shelly stepped onto the white mat and stared at herself in the foggy bathroom mirror. Water dripped from her hair and drops of moisture glistened on her freshly scrubbed skin. The bathroom in the motel was small, steamy now and barely big enough to accommodate her and her bag of toiletries.

Taking one of the fluffy white towels from the rack, she wound it around her head turban style, catching the short strands of hair so that the trickle of water no longer sluiced down the back of her neck. She reached for another towel to buff her naked body, but stopped as her fingers brushed the slightly damp bandage on her left arm. Wet, in spite of her efforts to keep that arm extended out of the water's reach.

She'd started her mission with a costly mistake, albeit one she'd had no control over. However, thinking back on the shooting incident now, she doubted Brady saw it that way. He hadn't chewed her out or removed her from the case yet, but when anything went wrong, he tended to blame the agent in charge. Screwups of any kind were not tolerated in his department.

But the plan was working. She was in control and even coming to terms with the sensual reactions Matt inspired. He possessed a masculine virility that personified the cowboy charm to perfection. She doubted there was a woman alive who wouldn't feel some sort of stirring in her soul when suddenly thrust up close and personal with him.

Add that to the fact that she'd been so busy learning the ropes at the agency, she hadn't been intimate with a man in months. She thought back. Make that a year and two months unless you counted those kisses with her senior-year boyfriend at her ten-year high school reunion last year. They'd been about as exciting as downing a spoonful of cough syrup.

Shelly finished drying and then slathered her skin with a slick coat of scented lotion. Moisturizer for her face came next, and there was no missing the paleness that made her skin look almost translucent in the glare of the overhead light. The wound and the loss of blood took a little more out of her than she'd wanted to admit, but a good night's sleep and she'd be just fine.

She pulled on the oversize nightshirt, turned out the light and padded to the bed. Fortunately, there had been lots of empty rooms at the motel and Matt had taken the one adjoining hers. The door that separated them was, at his insistence, open a crack. He'd double checked the locks on her door that opened directly to the parking lot and the ones on her small-paned window.

There was a soft tap on the adjoining door just as she slid beneath the covers. She yanked on the sheet, tucking the top folds of the smooth cotton beneath her armpits. "Come in."

Matt stepped inside, shirtless, his hair damp from the shower, his feet bare. His jeans rode his hips, the button at the waist was undone.

Her resolve to stay unmoved dissolved in a flash of heat. She turned to study the faded roses on the spread she'd pushed to the foot of the bed earlier.

Matt stepped even closer. "Are you too tired to talk a minute?"

"I'm exhausted, but I can probably stay awake for a sentence or two."

He leaned against the rough-hewn pine headboard. "I just had a call from Sheriff Guerra."

She let her hopes rise a little. "Have they apprehended the shooter?"

"Afraid not."

"Has he found out if anyone around here owns a car like the one my attacker was driving?"

"No. All they know is that a man in a black sedan bought gas in a local station less than a half hour before the attack on you. The owner was working at the station at the time and he took the man to be just passing through."

"When did you find that out?"

"Earlier this evening," he admitted.

"Why didn't you mention it before now?"

"Guess I forgot."

He hadn't forgotten. He didn't trust her. But he was here, protecting her though he owed her nothing. Could a man like that be guilty of selling out to the enemy? Or did he just have the misfortune to be born into a family that put money above moral decency and respect for innocent lives?

This was getting her nowhere. "What is it you wanted to talk about, Matt?"

"They haven't found the man who attacked you, but they may have found the car he was driving."

"When?"

"I'm not sure, but I just got the news. A wrangler from Gill Collin's ranch called in a report that he'd found a burning car. It was in a wooded area just past their south pasture. Ed Guerra called me as soon as he arrived on the scene and verified the report."

The name Gill Collin didn't register. She doubted it should

have. She took a deep breath and exhaled slowly. "Was there anyone in the car? Was it deliberately set on fire?"

"No one was in the car, but the sheriff is assuming at this point that the fire was deliberately set. The good news is the car wasn't burned to the point they couldn't recognize the VIN or that it was a black Ford Fusion. The sheriff ran a check on it. The car was reported as stolen from a grocery store in Conroe about an hour before the attack on you."

"So we're no closer to identifying the man who tried to kill me."

"Not unless you can come up with someone who might want you dead."

The Collingsworths would be the obvious first guess, yet she didn't think they were behind it. There were others with reason to hate her, but they were all behind bars and had been for months. People like the Maitlin brothers whom she'd helped send to prison for arms dealing.

Then there was Arthur Cox. He'd been involved with smuggling illegal aliens into the country, including one responsible for a failed bomb attack on an overseas military base.

Both Cox and the Maitlin brothers had sworn revenge, but she'd merely assisted in the investigations leading to their arrest. If they'd gone after anyone, it would have been the senior investigator, and that hadn't happened.

More importantly, no one knew she was here. Shelly Lane was a physical therapist from Atlanta with viable credentials and a fake background that was beyond suspicion. All she had to do now was convince Matt she was authentic.

"If the man was trying to kill me, Matt, then he had me confused with someone else. No one has a reason to hate me that much. I lead a quiet life."

Matt shifted, moving so near that she felt the pressure of

his thigh against her leg through the sheet. "I want to help you, Shelly, but I can't unless you level with me."

"I have leveled with you. I have no idea why anyone shot at me." She had to stay in control, had to think clearly and not let this get out of hand.

Matt's hand slid along the sheet until his fingertips touched hers. His touch was disconcerting, but nothing like the compelling heat of his eyes as he stared into hers. "You can trust me, you know. I have no stake in this, except to see that you don't get killed on my watch."

But *she* had a tremendous stake in this, and her job was all about digging into his secrets, not the other way around.

"If you need me, I'm just steps away, Shelly. All you have to do is call my name."

"You're surely not planning to stay awake waiting on some deranged killer to show up," she said.

"I'm a light sleeper. Now get some rest. We'll talk more in the morning."

She was exhausted, but when she closed her eyes and kicked back the covers, her knee settled in the warm spot left by Matt's body. She cringed and curled into a ball, hating that she found Matt attractive, but knowing that she'd do what she came to Texas to do—no matter what stunts her hormones pulled.

MATT WOKE FROM A RESTLESS sleep and stared at the shadows that crept about his walls and ceiling. If forced to explain his actions tonight, he'd be hard-pressed to come up with a good reason for assuming responsibility for the protection of a woman he'd just met and didn't totally trust.

Sure, there was an element of truth in his statement about family tradition and a real man always protecting a woman, but he could have called the sheriff and hired an off-duty deputy to stand guard over Shelly tonight. He'd considered doing just that, but when it came time to make the call, he couldn't turn the task over to anyone else. Far more disturbing were the urges that had rolled through him when he'd been sitting beside her on the bed.

He'd played it cool—at least he'd given it his best shot. For sure, he hadn't done anything irrevocably stupid like kissing her, but he'd come close. The possibility of danger and being with a woman in a dingy motel room was a lethal combination.

Giving up on sleep for the time being, he kicked out from under the bleached white sheet and threw his legs over the side of the bed. He took a bathroom break, then grabbed his jeans from the chair where he'd slung them and wiggled into them. He could use a breath of fresh air. Not that air ever seemed as fresh or as fragrant to him anywhere as it did on Jack's Bluff Ranch.

He was yanking up the zipper when he saw the shadow of a man move past his window. Maybe just a restless guest like himself, but caution kicked in and Matt grabbed the pistol from his beside table.

He eased the door open and stepped outside just in time to see a tall, thin man wearing a baseball cap lean over and start fiddling with the lock on Shelly's door.

The wind caught Matt's open door, slamming it shut and alerting the would-be intruder that he was there. The man glanced his way for less than a heartbeat before he took off running across the parking lot. Matt raced after him, his bare feet digging painfully into the uneven gravel and sending pebbles skittering in all directions.

He'd almost caught up with him when he heard a motorbike sputter then roar to life. As he turned toward the sound, something hit him square in the forehead. The pain was blinding and slowed him down just long enough for the man to jump on the back of the now-speeding bike.

Matt took aim with the pistol but there was no way he could get off a clean shot at the back tire with the driver weaving from one side of the road to the other. In seconds, they'd disappeared beyond the tree line.

He could jump in his truck and try to follow, but with their head start and the acres of wooded land they could cut through on their motorbike, there would be little chance he could catch them. A couple of motel lights came on, the illumination slanting through as guests peeked from behind cracked blinds. One man stepped outside in his underwear.

"Is that you making that ruckus?"

"Nope, I was just out for a smoke when a couple of guys on a Harley sped through the parking lot."

"So what happened to your head?"

Matt reached to the spot that felt as if someone had cracked it open with a two-by-four. A sticky pool of blood squished between his fingertips. "Guess a rock flying off his tire caught me." A major lie. The rock had definitely been hurled by a man with muscle and great aim.

The man's next comment wasn't fit for mixed company, but it pretty much summed up Matt's feelings about the bikers as well. That was the least disturbing facet of all of this. The most distressing was that one of the men had been at Shelly's door and who knows what he might have done if Matt hadn't been here.

His insides felt scratchy and gritty, the way they had that time he'd been stuck in that West Texas sandstorm. He stopped at Shelly's room and tried the knob of her door. The lock still held and her room was still dark. The meds and her state of exhaustion had probably let her sleep through everything.

Once inside his own space, he took a deep breath only to be struck by the suffocating sensation that the walls were closing in around him. He tiptoed to the door that separated his room from Shelly's and opened it enough that he could assure himself she was still sleeping soundly and safely.

Moonlight splayed across her bed, caressing her delicate features and painting silver threads along the column of her neck. Her eyes were closed, her breath even and gentle, as if she were in the deep throes of a pleasant dream.

She wasn't his responsibility, he reminded himself. He was a rancher, not a sheriff. He liked life uncomplicated and stress-free.

Still, there was something about Shelly Lane that burrowed inside him and made him feel hungry for something he couldn't even name. He didn't like the feeling at all.

MATT EXPLAINED THE SITUATION to Shelly over morning coffee he'd made in his motel room's pot. He'd probably had worse, but he couldn't remember when. She didn't complain about the coffee and seemed rather unfazed by his account of last night's adventure.

"I called the sheriff's department after I got back in my room," he continued after another gulp of the lukewarm brew. "The clerk took the information and said she'd pass it along to the deputies on duty in that area. Her inference was that they'd then be on the lookout for the two bikers. It was clear, however, that she didn't consider the incident emergency caliber."

"I can see her point," Shelly said. "The man didn't break into my room. He was just standing by my door. And you didn't have a rock thrown at you, until you started chasing the guy's friend across the parking lot." She sipped her coffee. "No guns were fired. No crime was committed. Thus, not emergency status."

"Apparently the sheriff's clerk thinks like you do. So does the motel manager for that matter. He said the guy was probably looking for someone, most likely a girlfriend he thought was running around with some other guy. Claims it's happened before, which says a lot for the quality of guests he gets at the motel."

"Well, if you're the only bed for hire in town you're bound to get some by-the-hour customers."

He knew she was right. That didn't change his mind about what he'd decided in the sleepless hours just before sunrise. "I need you to go into Houston with me today."

She stared at him over the rim of her cup. "For what purpose?"

"I have an artist friend there who's got a real talent for drawing faces from a description."

"You mean a police sketch artist?"

"No, she's better at it than any sketch artist the police can afford. She doesn't like becoming involved with criminal cases, but if she's available, she'll do it as a favor to me."

"I don't see how my seeing her would help. I didn't get a good look at the shooter."

"No, but if the shooter and the unidentified jerk who bought gas from Emile Henley are the same man, Emile can describe him. I just need you to see if the resulting sketch reminds you of anyone you know or have seen before."

"Don't you have duties with the behaviorally challenged?"

"I'll find a replacement. So, are you up for the trip?"

"If it will help us identify the lunatic who fired at me and destroyed a stolen car, how can I refuse?"

His sentiments exactly. As soon as they had an arrest and a full report on Shelly, he could go back to his life. In the meantime he'd just have to work doubly hard to keep his libido under control.

SHELLY WAS IN THE FRONT seat of Matt's truck traveling toward the service station to pick up Emile for the drive into Houston. Nothing was going according to plan, including the biker incident, but she had to concentrate on the positive.

She might not be on the ranch yet, but she was definitely getting closer.

"Tell me more about this artist," she said as Matt turned onto another two-lane highway. "Is she anyone I might have heard of?"

"Possibly. Her name's Angelique Dubois. I'm not much of an art critic, but she's regarded highly by the local art community."

"Not *the* Angelique Dubois who does the charcoals of nudes."

"That's the one. You sound as if you're familiar with her work."

She caught herself before she admitted that she'd gone to a showing of Angelique's drawings in the D.C. area just a few months ago. It didn't fit her Atlanta physical therapist's image. "I read an article about her on the Internet. I can't believe you got someone of her professional stature to do a police sketch for a low-profile crime."

"I called in a favor."

"How do you know her?" she asked.

"I met her when Mom dragged me to a charity event at a gallery that was showing her work. Actually, it was probably one of Mom's setups. Her primary goal in life lately seems to be to marry me off. Well, that and getting Jeremiah steady on his feet and out of the house more."

"Did the setup work?"

"Better than most. Angelique and I dated a few times."

"But you're not dating now?" Just making conversation,

she told herself, but she tensed involuntarily as she waited for his response.

"No. She didn't particularly warm up to ranch life and I took to her world even less. We stayed friends, though, and I sent a rich buyer her way last month, a ranching friend from Australia."

The Collingsworths had rich friends in every corner of the globe, and Shelly was about to make her first step into that world of wealth, influence, social contacts and even art.

She needed to apprise Brady of her current status at her first opportunity. He'd be wary when she told him about the unexplained bikers, but he'd have to see that she was making too much headway to pull her off the case now.

Matt turned on his CD player and a jazzy instrumental blared from the truck's speakers. She would have expected him to listen to country, though she wasn't sure why. He hadn't fallen into any of the other wealthy Texas rancher stereotypical slots she might have assigned him.

Shelly shifted, so that she could study the angles and strong features of his profile as they talked. "Is ranching as romantic as it seems in books?"

"All depends on which books you read and which day you're on the ranch."

Matt nudged his white straw Stetson away from his forehead, and thick, dark locks of hair crept from beneath the brim, skimming the angry wound from last night's rock injury. Not his only scar, though. There was an almost invisible one running along his left temple.

His jaw was chiseled, his nose classic, his chest broad. Even his scent was masculine, a hint of spice and seductive musk. Her pulse quickened. Not what she needed to be thinking about.

"What's a typical day like for you?" she asked, hoping conversation would keep more sensual thoughts at bay.

Matt kept his left hand on the wheel, but snaked his arm across the space between them, resting his right hand near her shoulder. "The day starts at sunrise when I step out on my porch and get that first invigorating whiff of fresh air. Birds serenade me from the trees around the house and there's a good chance I'll spy deer drinking from the pond. Might even see a fish jump and see a family of ducks out for a morning swim.

"After a few minutes, I'll amble back inside and start a pot of real coffee—not like what we drank this morning—while I go over the day's agenda in my mind."

"No calendar of activities or a secretary to keep you on task."

"I have a calendar. I seldom need to refer to it. We have a staff to handle reports and finances, but they work out of the headquarters building near the wranglers' bunkhouse. Bart and I both spend as little time in there as we can. Fortunately, we have people for the paperwork who need little supervision and don't mind being cooped up for several hours a day."

"Then what kind of duties are on your agenda?"

"A colt about to be born. Branding that needs to be done. Decisions to make about what types of cattle to increase and which to cut back on. Auctions to attend. New equipment to check out. Wranglers to oversee."

He retuned his right hand to the wheel. "I guess that sounds corny to a city girl."

"Not at all," she murmured. It sounded earthy and real, far removed from the world of crime and national security she dealt with every day. "Do you have much involvement with Collingsworth Oil?" she asked.

"Almost none."

"But it is a family business, isn't it?"

"It is, but we all do what makes us happy. We're lucky that

way. My brother Bart and I run the ranch. My brother Langston is president of the oil company and my youngest brother Zach is going into law enforcement when he gets back from his honeymoon."

"How did Langston end up with so much control of the oil business?"

"He likes it. So did Jeremiah when he was on top of his mental game. The rest of us don't, although Mom is doing a bang-up job of CEO of Collingsworth Enterprises since Jeremiah had to step down from the position. I think she's growing tired of it though and is ready to return to her charities and grandmothering."

"But you must at least go to board meetings for the oil company?"

"The annual meeting, but only because Langston insists that we all know the financial status of the business." He turned toward her. "Why are you so interested in Collingsworth Oil?"

She pulled down the visor and checked her lipstick, giving her a reason to avoid eye contact with Matt. "This kind of life is all new to me. Besides, listening to you helps keep my mind off my wounded arm and battered car."

"I'll take care of the car. You'll have to rely on the doc for your arm. When do you need to get it checked again?"

"Today, but it can wait until after we visit with Angelique."

Matt nodded, then slowed the car and pulled into a three-pump service station accompanied by what looked to be a country mini-mart.

A man in faded jeans and a black T-shirt waved to them from the open doorway of the store.

"I need to use the facilities," she said, realizing that this might be her only opportunity to make a quick phone call to Brady.

"Okay, I'll wait here. Bathrooms are inside to your left, past the drink machines."

She threw her handbag over her shoulder and hopped down from the truck. Emile was giving last-minute instructions to the young man who was apparently going to watch the station while they made the trip into Houston. Once inside the bathroom, she used the CIA phone to make a call to Brady's private, non-traceable line, hoping for decent reception. He answered on the second ring.

"Good news and bad," she said.

"Hit me with it—the bad first."

She told him about the visit of the moonlight biker before explaining that Matt had taken on her protection as his personal responsibility. "He's concerned because he thinks someone is trying to kill me, proof positive that he has no clue that I'm with the CIA."

"There's no such thing as that kind of proof in this business. Don't take anything for granted, Shelly."

"Absolutely not." But Matt wouldn't be doing all this if he thought she was here to investigate his family. He'd just fire her, and that would be that.

"I'd feel better if I was certain the attack was random and the biker visit was unrelated."

"I'm Shelly Lane, a physical therapist from Atlanta. No one has a reason to kill me. If it wasn't random, the perp has me mixed up with someone else. He'll realize that soon enough. But most likely it's some weird gang-related activity."

"That's possible. Gang-related violence has been up in Houston ever since so many of the druggies fled New Orleans after Katrina."

"I'm already making headway with Matt Collingsworth, Brady. It would be a shame to get pulled off the case before I have a chance to try my skills with the rest of the family."

"You don't have anything on Matt yet."

"That's the point. I don't think he's involved in the workings of the oil company. Indications are that he's all rancher, all the time."

"I hate to burst that bubble of self-confidence, but there's new evidence to the contrary."

She leaned against the stained sink, pretty sure she did not want to hear what was going to come next.

Chapter Six

"Agents picked up a man last night in Brownsville, Texas, who is known to have ties with terrorist organizations in the Middle East. The CIA's been watching him for a while, but couldn't get the goods on him until he was caught smuggling illegal aliens across the Mexican border. At least two of the men he brought into the country were from Middle Eastern countries and had ties with the Taliban."

"How is that related to Matt Collingsworth?"

"When he was arrested, he had Matt's name and phone number on him. He claimed not to know any of the Collingsworths, but said he'd been given Matt's name as someone who hired illegals."

"That's possible, I guess, but Lenora Collingsworth certainly checked my credentials thoroughly and is having me further investigated now."

"More reason to suspect that Matt's dealings with the man involved more than he claimed. At this point, we have to assume that any family member might be involved in illegal activities and those who aren't might still have information that can lead us to arrests and convictions."

And there was even an outside chance—way outside at this point—that none of the evidence they had against any of the Collingsworth family would check out. Brady knew it, but would not want to hear that from her. She broke the connection and went to rejoin Matt.

He looked the same, but she saw him differently than she had mere minutes ago. Then, she'd let him slide into the role of protector, let herself start relaxing in his presence and experience twinges of attraction deep inside her psyche.

Now, Matt Collingsworth was just one more important piece of the criminal puzzle she had to solve. There was no room for mistakes in judgment. No room for mistakes of any kind.

ANGELIQUE DUBOIS MET THEM at the door of her quaint turn-of-the-century house in Houston's Heights district, wearing a pair of extremely skinny jeans and a flowing teal blouse. She was absolutely gorgeous. Take that back. The word didn't do her justice. She was positively ethereal, like a goddess floating on a sea of off-white carpet.

Her black hair was straight and sleek and hung nearly to her waist. Her olive complexion was flawless. Her skin was bronzed with a natural glow that required no makeup though there was a glimmer of gloss on her full lips and a smidgen of berry-colored liner at the base of her long, thick lashes.

Her eyes were the real kicker—intense, the color of polished onyx. And they were staring up at Matt with the kind of overt hunger that Shelly might have reserved for a pair of Manolo Blahniks about to go on the half-price sale rack.

Emile shuffled his feet and stared at his grease-stained hands and dirty nails, as if noticing them for the first time, as Matt took care of introductions. Finally, he offered his right hand to Angelique.

She shook his quickly and turned to Shelly. "I'm sorry that

your welcome to Texas was so traumatic. Matt said you narrowly missed being killed yesterday."

"But luckily I got off with barely a scratch," she said, patting the bandage on her arm. "I really appreciate your willingness to lend your expertise in finding my attacker."

"Matt asked for my help," Angelique said as if that were explanation enough. "Can I get you something to drink? Hot tea or there's chilled champagne if you'd prefer a mimosa. And, yes, there's coffee, Matt. I knew you'd want that."

"Great. You know what I think of champagne."

"Lacks the proper kick and should be reserved for momentous occasions and boring toasts. I think that's how you put it," she said, laughing.

"Close enough. Who else wants coffee?"

Shelly and Emile put in their orders for black and unsweetened. Matt and Angelique went to fetch the brew while Shelly took in the ambiance. The furnishings were comfortable and reminiscent of the same period as the house, but accessorized with a mixture of jewel-toned colors that mimicked brilliant sunrises and Caribbean seas.

Shelves and tables were adorned with unique sculptures, books and small, framed photographs in black-and-white. An unframed charcoal canvas of a shapely young woman strategically draped in what appeared to be the folds of a curtain she'd pulled away from a window hung over the mantle.

"Is that your work?" Shelly asked, when Angelique returned carrying a silver tray laden with thinly sliced sweet breads and pastries.

"Yes. Do you like it?"

"It's intriguing," she said. "I love the way the shadows and shadings give it that fantasized feel. Forgive my layman's terms for describing what's probably a very sophisticated artistic method."

"No need to apologize. Vocabulary is unimportant. The artist's purpose is to portray an image that can touch the soul."

"Beautifully put."

"I'd love to paint you," Angelique said. "Your face is a fascinating blend of strength and vulnerability, and your body is lissome and sensual."

Shelly's face burned at the thought of nude modeling, not to mention the fact that she'd never thought of her body as lissome or sensual. When she looked up and realized Matt had returned and also heard the comment, the blush burned even deeper into her cheeks.

"Thanks," Shelly said, "but I'm uncomfortable enough having my photograph taken with my clothes *on*."

"If you change your mind, you know where to find me. Now, I guess we should get started on the sketch. Emile, you sit on the sofa next to me and try to picture the man just as he looked when he walked into your store."

"I can try."

"It will be easier than you think. Just close your eyes and relive the moment in your mind. When the image is intact, open your eyes and start describing him. I'll interrupt with questions as you talk and you should speak up when my sketch veers from the way you see him."

"I only saw the man for a few minutes."

"But you probably noticed more than you think you did. The mind captures images we're not aware of seeing." Angelique picked up the sketch pad and pencil she'd left lying on the coffee table. She settled on the far end of the Queen Anne sofa. Emile sat next to her. Shelly took her coffee to the loveseat opposite them, afraid after she did that Matt would likely take that as an invitation to join her there. He grabbed one of the pastries and a napkin, then did just that.

This time, Shelly managed to keep his nearness from overriding her professional judgment. The possibility that she might recognize the man Angelique was about to sketch had her on edge for very good reasons. If it turned out to be someone she knew, it would mean she was the target of a planned hit. In that case, not only would she be in danger of being ambushed and shot at again, but it would mean her cover was indisputably blown.

Emile began to describe the man, speaking slowly and awkwardly at first, but he gained momentum quickly as the sketch started to take shape.

"His chin was square."

"Like this?" Angelique said, making the adjustment.

"Yeah, that's more like it, and his brows were thicker with some hairs shooting out all whichaway, like a porcupine's."

Angelique changed the drawing until Emile was satisfied with the brows and the hair. "What about the mouth?"

"He had big lips, blotchy, you know, like he'd had cold sores recently."

Angelique went through the same process with the mouth, changing the lines until Emile nodded.

"That's starting to look like him," he said.

"Tell me about his eyes."

"Oh, boy. A man never looks at another man's eyes."

"Let's give it a try anyway."

"Kind of mean-looking."

"Check this shape," she said. Her perfectly manicured fingers seemed to move effortlessly across the pad.

Emile frowned. "Try making them narrower, and with the lids down, like they weren't open all the way."

She made the adjustments. The sketch was definitely not of the man Shelly had noticed staring at her at Cutter's Bar last night. It was even possible that the sketch didn't resemble the man in the black Ford at all. That had happened more than once with the sketch agents they'd used at the agency and they had access to people trained in transferring verbal descriptions to the blank page.

Angelique kept at the task, making minute modifications until Emile finally broke into a broad grin.

"I don't know how you did it from my rambling, but that's him to a T. You're amazing."

"I just drew what you said." Angelique tore the sketch from the pad and handed the drawing to Matt. "I hope this helps."

He scooted closer to Shelly and held it so that she could study it with him. His arm brushed hers and awareness zinged through her, in spite of the gravity of the situation. This whole attraction bit was starting to become extremely annoying. She forced her total concentration on the sketch.

"I've never see him around Colts Run Cross," Matt said.

"Just like I told you yesterday," Emile said, appearing far more relaxed, now that he was off the hook. "I don't think he's from around here."

"What's the verdict, Shelly?" Matt laid a hand on her arm. "Do you know him?"

She shook her head. "I've never seen him before."

"You're sure?" Suspicion haunted his voice and his eyes.

"I'm sure."

"Then I guess we'll just turn this sketch over to Sheriff Guerra and let him get it out to law-enforcement personnel across the state. The quicker this guy is arrested, the less likely he'll attack someone else, randomly or otherwise."

Angelique walked them to the door, stopping after she opened it to straighten Matt's shirt collar, though it wasn't crooked. Her delicate hand lingered on his chest, a seductive gesture that didn't go unnoticed by Shelly, but seemed to fly right past Matt. His only interest appeared to be in getting the sketch into the sheriff's hands.

Or maybe it was to just deliver her back to the motel and get on with his life. Either way, they made a quick exit. The drive back to Colts Run Cross was an hour and a half of awkward silence, except for occasional bursts of conversation between Matt and Emile.

Her entrée into the Collingsworth household might be about to run into a dead end.

MATT PACED THE HOSPITAL waiting room, while the young doctor on Saturday call examined the wound and then had the nursing staff change the bandage.

Matt's cell phone rang. He grabbed it, hoping it was the sheriff telling him the sketch had produced an identification. Probably way too soon for that now, though. They'd dropped off the sketch less than a half hour ago and picked up Shelly's gun while they were there. She'd handled the weapon like a pro, not like a woman who'd just bought a gun for a long road trip.

The caller ID said Langston. "I thought you were replacing me," Matt said. "Why aren't you saddling horses for the visiting inner-city brood?"

"As usual, Mom has twice the volunteers she needs so I slipped away to take care of some business. Are you still with Shelly Lane?"

"Yeah. Angelique completed the sketch, but Shelly says the likeness doesn't resemble anyone she knows."

"That would fit with the news from Clay Markham? So far our physical therapist checks out perfectly. And Aidan talked with a fellow detective who works for the Atlanta Police Department."

"Always nice to have friends in high places."

"And sometimes in low places. Aidan has both. He says

Shelly has never reported any safety concerns to the police, nor is there a record of her having ever made a 911 call. From all indications, she's a model citizen with no reported stalkers or danger in her background."

"Are you saying I should just bring her to the ranch as Mom's wanted all along?"

"I don't see any real problem with it, but you're with Shelly. You decide."

Making the call *should* be a simple task. Shelly insisted that no one had reason to kill her. The cops and private investigators had no evidence that she was in any kind of trouble or mixed up in any way with killers.

But Matt had always had a sixth sense with cattle. He knew from looking in a cow's eyes when her pregnancy was going sour. He knew if a calf or foal was unhealthy, almost before it's feet touched the ground. Shelly wasn't livestock, but all his instincts yelled that she was in danger.

Not that he knew a damn thing about women, except that the status quo usually flew out the window when a woman like Shelly stepped onto the scene. And he liked his status quo. He was still dealing with that fact, when Shelly and the doctor joined him in the waiting room.

"You'll have your hands full with this one, Mr. Collingsworth."

"Are there complications?"

"Not with the injury, but Shelly does not follow doctor's orders. She skipped out without being released last night and today she's telling me how to do my job."

It was clear he was joking, probably flirting with Shelly. Maybe he'd be willing to take her home with him? Then Matt's life could get back to normal.

"You look as if you took a blow yourself?" the doctor said, stepping closer for a better look at the cut on Matt's forehead.

"It's nothing a little time and a smear of antibiotic cream won't take care of. What's the verdict with Shelly's wound?" Matt asked, almost hoping the doctor wanted her back in the hospital. That would eliminate his having to make any decision on what to do with her tonight. But from the size of the much smaller bandage on her arm now, he'd guess that wasn't going to happen.

"I prescribed an ointment to be used twice a day, in the morning and at night before changing the bandage. Keeping the wound clean is very important, so she should keep it bandaged until Tuesday. I should see her in seven days. We'll remove the stitches then."

"I could probably remove the stitches myself," Shelly said, "since I don't have a car at my disposal."

The doctor looked to Matt. "It would be better if she had that done in the office. That way we can make certain the wound is healing appropriately."

"I'll see that she comes in," Matt said. It didn't hit him until after he'd blurted out the words that they sounded as if he and Shelly were a couple and he would still be taking care of her a week from now.

That, coupled with the plan taking form in his mind, rattled him to the point that he almost dropped the keys when he went to unlock his truck. The plan wasn't to his liking, but he didn't see much else he could do, unless he wanted to spend another sleepless night in the motel.

"You really don't need to babysit me any longer, Matt," she said, as if reading his confusing thoughts. "Just drop me off at the motel. I'll be fine. And if a drunk biker comes calling in the middle of the night, I have my gun that the sheriff returned."

"The gun you admitted you don't know how to use."

"What's to know? You just aim and pull the trigger. I've seen it done in a thousand movies."

He backed out of the parking lot and turned right, toward the motel. He couldn't believe he was about to say what was bucking around in his mind and fighting its way to his tongue.

"We'll stop off at the motel and pick up your things."

Shelly's brows arched and the golden flecks in her eyes sparkled like fire. His insides felt vaguely the way they had when he'd been kicked in the gut by a snorting bull, all shaky and queasy. But he had to do what he had to do.

"I think it best you stay with me tonight," he said.

"You mean stay at the ranch?"

"Yes, but at my house." His small, rustic, cozy cabin that he was used to living in alone. "Just until tomorrow," he said, before she got the wrong idea, like the one that was messing with his libido right now.

"Is this your mother's idea or yours?"

"Mine."

"Because you still don't trust me to live with your family?"

He couldn't deny the truth of that, but admitting it would only make things worse. "Because the investigation isn't finished."

The sparks in her eyes seemed to be shooting at him now. "Then I'll wait until it is."

She had a lot of nerve being angry with him after he'd spent the past twenty-four hours trying to make sure she was safe. He had a good mind to dump her at that motel and go home to his nice, comfortable bed alone.

Nice thought, but he could no more walk away and leave her unprotected than he could have decided to stop breathing. He wouldn't even try to understand why he'd let her get to him this way. She just had.

The problem was that those nagging doubts of suspicion

wouldn't die. And he wasn't willing to move her into the big house until he felt certain she wasn't into anything that would bring trouble or danger to his family.

"It's your call, but we'd both be more comfortable than at the motel. You'd have a modern bathroom and an air conditioner that doesn't buck and whistle all night. And we could join the family for brunch in the morning," he said, hoping that would sway her. "You can meet Jeremiah."

Shelly cocked her head and shot Matt a dubious look. "Does this house of yours have two bedrooms?"

"Actually it has three. And if you're worried that I plan to take advantage of you, forget it. When I take a woman to bed, it's because she wants to be there."

She stretched her feet in front of her and pushed against the back of the seat, the movement accentuating her perky breasts.

"Okay, Matt Collingsworth, on those grounds, I accept your invitation to stay with you tonight."

He swallowed hard, glad he'd won the argument, but worried at the same time. He'd keep his word, but he had a feeling this might well be a night for a cold shower.

Chapter Seven

Shelly had seen pictures of the ranch, had even driven by it when she'd first arrived in Texas, but that hadn't quite prepared her for this. A lump formed in her throat as the reality and significance of the moment hit home.

She was about to be on-site, undercover and officially on a case that, if successful, might save thousands of innocent lives. Who knew what reprehensible and deadly acts might be committed using money funneled to terrorists through Collingsworth Oil? All for the purpose of making even more money for a family who were already worth billions.

Her sense of responsibility swelled as Matt punched in a code and the gates swung open. But she couldn't let Matt discern those feelings. She had to stay firmly planted in her role of a Georgia girl who knew nothing much about the Collingsworths or the ranch.

"Nice gate, but I always pictured cowboys climbing down from a battered pickup and unlatching a rusty latch."

"Sorry to disappoint you. But if it's any consolation, the automated gate opener is new, part of the added security after a year of dealing with lunatics."

Her interest piqued. She knew something of the problems his new sisters-in-law had experienced, but it would be nice to hear Matt's version of them. "Then you've had other trouble?"

"Long stories for winter nights by the fire. But all the endings were happy."

"After the way everyone reacted to the attack on me," she continued, "I would have thought there was no crime in this part of Texas."

"Crime is everywhere these days, but we don't get the kind of drug and gang-related crimes they get in big cities or along the border. Unfortunately, the Collingsworth brothers do have a knack for getting linked with women in jeopardy."

"Do tell. More of the cowboy code at work?"

"You could say that. Our neighbor Billy Mack calls it the Lenora Do-gooder Curse. Mom's constantly quoting from the Bible parable about how to whom much is given, much is required. Guess she has that so drilled into our brains that, when we see someone who needs help, we feel compelled to rush to the rescue."

"That explains her having the inner-city kids out for a day of ranch life? Does she do that often?"

"Every other Saturday during the summer months. We all pitch in, wranglers included, but she has lots of volunteers from neighboring ranches as well."

"How many kids are we talking about?"

"No more than twelve at a time, all between the ages of eleven and fourteen. Mom insists that each kid have their own adult mentor for the day. Mostly that's for safety reasons, but also because she says that, for some of them, it's the only time they have an adult's full attention—unless they're with a cop or a judge."

"Cops and judges. So you're talking about kids with serious problems?"

"Sometimes."

"How does she decide which kids to include?"

"Her friend Carolyn Kenny does it for her. She's a juvenile court judge in Houston."

Shelly knew the Collingsworth family were major financial backers of several charitable organizations, but this was more than just a donation. They brought these kids into their world and gave them individual attention. Billionaires out riding horses with delinquents. It wasn't what she'd expected to find.

Shelly tried to reconcile what she'd seen firsthand of the Collingsworths, especially Matt, with what the CIA believed to be true about them. It refused to gel.

That didn't change her reason for being here or her motive for worming her way into their lives. "Your mother sounds amazing. You have a lot to live up to."

"Tell me about it. I respect what Mom does, but I'm not that good with people myself. Give me horses and cows any day. If they turn on you, it's because you gave them a reason."

They continued down a smooth blacktop road surrounded by acres and acres of a pastoral countryside that epitomized tranquility and the American West. She wasn't sure exactly what she'd expected the ranch to be like, but so far, it seemed the setting for a romance novel. Green and open and inviting.

"Those are longhorns in the pasture to your left," Matt said, slowing for her to get a better look.

A half dozen cattle were clustered near the fence and Shelly turned to peer out the window for her first up-close view of the huge animals with their vicious-looking horns. One looked up as if knowing it were on display; it seemed proud to show off its armor.

"How long are those horns?"

"For a steer they can measure up to a hundred and twenty

inches tip to tip. Cows and bulls have shorter horns, but a seventy to eighty inch tip range isn't uncommon. The ones you're looking at now are cows."

"Is your herd primarily Texas longhorns?"

"No. They make up only about a fourth of our herd at the present time, but I keep adding more. Hook 'em horns."

"Should I know what that means?"

He slapped the butt of his hand against his temple as if she'd offended him. "Longhorns are the University of Texas mascot. Hook 'em horns is the school battle cry."

"And I take it you graduated from UT."

"Yep. And proud of it."

"How many types of cattle do you raise?"

"Six, though our main beef-producing stock is Santa Gertrudis. They do well in hot, humid environments. But we're constantly researching genetic improvements within our herds."

Matt swerved to miss a turtle that was lumbering across the road.

"He's huge," she said.

Matt grinned. "Haven't you noticed? Everything's bigger and better in Texas."

Whether he meant it to or not, the comment concocted a sensual image that sent a traitorous tingle of responsiveness dancing along her nerve endings. "So I've heard," she said, hating that she could feel the heat settling in her cheeks.

They drove in silence, as the road meandered away from fenced pasture land into a wooded area where towering pines intermingled with sweet gum, oak and birch.

A baby deer with a smooth spotted coat and long spindly legs stepped into a clearing near the edge of the road. Matt slowed to a stop a few yards away. Amazingly, the fawn stood still, head high, looking right at them. Shelly stared back until the fawn turned away and disappeared back into the cover of trees and brush.

"He was beautiful," Shelly said. "And he didn't even seem wary of us."

"Because we don't allow hunting on the ranch. Does make regular visits to the pond behind my house. They're so tame, they'll wonder right up to me. But then I spoil them a bit by putting out corn for them during the winter."

Ranch life was becoming more enticing by the moment. So was the rancher sitting next to Shelly—and therein lay the problem. Matt might seem too good to be true, but he was a suspect in her investigation.

She held on to that thought, until he rounded yet another curve in the road and a massive, rambling house came into view. The wooden structure was painted white with dark green shutters. Huge clay pots of blooming begonias and hanging baskets of bougainvillea provided a riot of summer color to the wide front porch.

The whole effect was picture-book Southern ranch right down to the swing that was currently occupied by a beautiful dark-haired woman who looked as if she might be ready to deliver a baby at any moment.

"That's the big house," Matt said.

"It's incredibly…" She struggled for a word to describe the sensations the house stirred.

"It's home," Matt said, putting it into the one word that said it all. "My brothers and I all have our own places, but the big house is still the center of all the family activities. You'll see that for yourself tomorrow morning. Family Sunday brunch is a long-standing tradition."

The woman in the porch swing looked up and waved as they passed. Matt waved back.

"Is that one of your sisters-in-law?"

"That's Langston's wife, Trish. You'll love her. Everyone does. She's expecting a baby boy within the next few weeks."

Trish was having a baby with a man Shelly was here to help send to jail. The information that helped seal the deal might even come from Trish during a casual conversation with the new physical therapist. It could just be a comment in passing that Shelly would gather for the CIA—a piece to the complex puzzle that would lead to conviction.

The irony of it bothered Shelly, but she couldn't let herself get caught up in guilt when she was only doing her job. Her gaze moved away from the house, to the stables off to the left. A half dozen magnificent horses lazed in a fenced area just beyond that.

"Do you ride?" Matt asked.

"A little." But only because she'd had lessons in preparation for this assignment. "I've never been around horses much and I find them a bit intimidating."

"We have some gentle mares that will break you in easy— if you stay."

It was clear he had not fully accepted that possibility yet. They reached open pastureland again and the ranch seemed to stretch for miles, mostly flat. "Where is the bluff?"

"Bluff?"

"Jack's Bluff."

"Oh, that." A smile claimed his mouth. "Different kind of bluff. My great, great grandfather who'd arrived in America penniless, won the original ranch in a game of poker. His winning hand was a pair of jacks, hence Jack's Bluff."

"He won all of this in a card game?"

"No, he won a patch of land that for the most part hadn't been cleared. He and succeeding generations of Collingsworths made the ranch and the oil company what it is today. You'll have to get Mom to tell you the story of how it all came about. It always sounds a lot more romantic when she explains it."

A tale of rags to riches. A family determined to forge ahead and find wealth in the rough and tumble world of Texas. That would take courage, ambition and possibly a willingness to bend all the rules. Maybe that was also a part of the Collingsworth heritage.

The truck bumped along, the woods growing deeper, the road to Matt's cabin more narrow and not as smoothly paved as the road to the big house had been. "That's it," Matt said, as his cabin came into view.

Shelly loved it at once. Where the big house had been large and rambling, Matt's cabin put her in mind of Goldilocks and the three bears. The house was stone and wood, interesting but non-assuming. It fit so well in its environment that it almost seemed an extension of nature's beauty.

Matt stopped and killed the truck's engine. "Welcome to my little corner of the ranch."

His private space. And he was about to usher her inside. A traitorous anticipation danced along her nerve endings and she feared it had nothing to do with the real reason she was here. She couldn't let herself start thinking of Matt as a man. He was a suspect. And she was here to find evidence that could send him to prison for a long, long time.

EVERYTHING WAS PERFECT. Nothing was right.

Matt knew who he was and where he belonged. It was as clear as the shine on his boots. Shelly had been in the same boat, just as sure, just as confident—until he'd stepped into her life. Now she vacillated between resolute dedication to her job and feeling as if she were setting up the pope for a prison term.

The CIA had valid evidence, collected over a period of months, all of it pointing to the Collingsworths—Matt included—as being guilty of funding terrorism. The latest evidence suggested that they might even be actively involved in smuggling dangerous illegals into the country.

So why was it that Shelly was finding it so difficult to believe Matt could be guilty? Surely she wasn't swayed by the singular fact that she found him attractive. She wasn't that shallow or nearly that unprofessional. Yet he did get to her on a sensual level.

She walked to the window of Matt's guest room and watched the setting sun. The room was comfortable, the queen-size iron bed covered in a beautiful quilt that looked as if it might have been handed down for generations.

A rustic, antique desk topped with a brass lamp and supplied with writing essentials sat against one wall. A forty-five inch television hung on the opposite wall, in dramatic contrast with the pine boot bench that sat below it. A mixture of old and new, of ranch tradition and modern technology. The same kind of contrast that personified Matt's personality.

He not only looked the part, but played the role of simple cowboy to perfection while talking of genetic improvements and socializing with seductive, esteemed artists.

But neither his self-assurance nor his complexity were what had her cocooning in the guest room for the last two hours. Nor was it the need for rest as she'd told Matt. The quandary was that the attraction she felt toward him had magnified since arriving on the ranch.

If she couldn't work her way past it soon, she'd have no ethical choice except to walk away from the assignment. Brady would view that as failure of the worst kind. The other agents would agree. And the last thing Shelly needed in her life was failure. She was a solid career woman. The CIA was her life.

She turned at a light knock at her door, then crossed the room and opened it.

Matt had changed into a short-sleeve knit shirt and a pair of khaki shorts. No boots. In fact, no shoes. But even without the western attire, he reeked of virility.

"Are you hungry? Potatoes are baking, the salad's made and steaks are ready for the grill."

"I could have helped."

"You can have kitchen cleanup duty."

"Deal. I'll be with you in a minute."

"Take your time. I'll decant the wine. My selection's not that great but I have a couple of cabernets or a pinot noir that I bought on a trip to Napa. I've been saving it for a special occasion."

"Then you shouldn't waste it."

"I wouldn't be. Cooking dinner for a woman happens rarely enough with me for it to classify as an occasion."

"Then I vote for the pinot." And for a night where nothing heated up but the grill, a significant breakthrough in the case would be nice, too.

She brushed some gloss on her lips, bronzed her cheeks and checked her reflection in the mirror one last time. She'd slipped into a pair of white shorts that did nice things for her tanned legs, and an azure cotton shirt that was gathered at the neckline, skimming her breasts before falling loose to her waist. Her white, strappy sandals buckled at the ankle.

Not too sexy. Not too dowdy. Low-key worked best for an undercover agent.

Satisfied with her appearance, she joined Matt in the kitchen where he was pouring wine into glasses. He handed her one and lifted his for a toast. "To a quick arrest of the suspect," he said, "and a fast recovery for you."

She touched her glass to his, then sipped the wine before settling on a leather and wood barstool.

"The potatoes need another thirty minutes. What do you

say we take our wine down to the pond until it's time to grill the filets?"

She nodded, then turned to a collection of snapshots that were clustered on the wall of the breakfast nook.

"Angelique helped me put that display together," Matt said. "She's big into black-and-white pictures and she thought I had too many bare walls."

Cooking dinner for women might be a rare occurrence, but she'd bet he'd cooked for Angelique. But somehow she couldn't see the sultry artist settling for the guest room.

Jealousy reared its ugly head. Shelly pulled her lips taut and ignored it, turning her attention back to the snapshots. They were mostly of Matt and his brothers; all were faces she recognized from her research.

"Is that you in the football uniform?"

"Yep. Quarterback for the Colts Run Cross Cougars, circa twenty years in the past. I was in the seventh grade."

Even then he'd been cute. The man with his arm around Matt wasn't half bad, either. "Who's that with you?"

"My dad. That was taken in the fall. He was killed the next spring. It was the last picture the two of us were in together."

"How was he killed?"

"He was a helicopter pilot with the Air National Guard. His chopper went down during routine training maneuvers. The only explanation we ever got was that there was an equipment failure. One day he was the center of all our lives. The next day he was dead."

"That must have been hard on all of you."

"Yeah, but especially on Mom, I think. She had six kids to take care of. My youngest brother and sister are twins and they hadn't even started first grade."

"She must have been furious with the government when he died so needlessly."

"Mom? Furious with the government? I don't think that ever entered her mind. As far as she's concerned, Dad is a hero who died serving his country."

"Do you think that way, too?"

"Yeah." He answered quickly, as if he'd given this a lot of thought before tonight. "I don't agree with every politician who runs his mouth off to get a few votes, but I believe in America. I believe in freedom and in doing whatever it takes to preserve it. I know that may sound corny."

"It doesn't sound corny at all."

Nor did it sound like a man who'd sell out to the enemy. Dichotomous thoughts flooded her mind, hitting with such intensity they left her dizzy. Couldn't Matt just once do or say something to make her job easier?

"Are you sure you feel like walking down to the pond?"

"I feel fine."

"You just looked a little pale there for a minute."

"Must be the wine on an empty stomach."

They both knew she was lying since she'd only had a sip, but he let the subject drop. He held the back door open for her, then walked beside her down a worn path that trailed from his back door to a pond bordered by towering pines.

"Mornings and dusk are the best times of day on the ranch," he said. "It's when the daytime, dusk and nocturnal creatures cross paths. The clearings around the pond come alive with activity."

Somehow the thought of being surrounded by wild animals, even small ones, didn't seem as appealing to her as it apparently did to Matt. "We're not taking snakes, I hope."

"You can't live in Texas without seeing an occasional snake."

"Then make sure they know I'm just visiting."

A tree frog chorus began a high-pitched serenade. A bull

frog filled in with alto chords. And a couple of jays squawked at them from a distance. They had almost reached the pond, when she spotted the heron. It swooped to the bank and balanced perfectly on one strawlike leg.

She was still staring at it in awe when the first of Matt's nightly parade of deer appeared at the edge of a shadowed clearing. This time it was a magnificent buck with impressive antlers and soulful eyes.

Shelly held her breath so long it burned in her lungs. She didn't want to make any move that would frighten him away. She needn't have worried. The buck looked right at her, then walked to the edge of the pond and drank from the clear blue water. Three graceful does joined him a few moments later.

"No wonder you love it here, cowboy."

Matt responded with an arm around her shoulder. She turned and met his gaze. A bad move. The moment of awe she'd been experiencing was swallowed up by an ache that seemed to hit every cell of her being at once.

Matt was too alive, too masculine, *too near.* His lips touched hers—just a brush, as if he were testing the waters.

She sank into his kiss and the sweet, salty taste of his lips was like an elixir for the soul. She wanted to drown in his kiss, to hold him so tight she could feel every twinge of his muscles and sink her fingertips in smooth flesh of his broad shoulders.

She'd never wanted anything more, but—

It was all wrong. Very, very wrong. She yanked away so fast she stumbled backward.

Matt caught and steadied her. "I'm sorry, Shelly. I didn't mean for that to happen. It…"

He was fumbling for words. She was struggling just to keep from throwing herself back into his arms. "It's okay, Matt," she said, her voice strained from the breath-stealing kiss. "You just surprised me. That's all."

He nodded, but his gaze stayed locked with hers. Whatever she was feeling, she had to get over it fast. She positively could not let him kiss her again. Not because Brady would care as long as it got useful information. But because she refused to want Matt in that way.

Matt pushed his hands into the front pockets of his shorts. "I overstepped the boundaries," he said. "You can relax. I promise I won't touch you again."

Good, because she wasn't crazy about having her willpower put to the test again.

Chapter Eight

"Grandma, Derrick kicked me under the table."

"Did not." The boy's denial was accompanied by a mischievous smirk.

"Did, too."

"Don't kick your brother, Derrick."

"Pass that sausage gravy down this way before you set it down, Bart."

"This bisque is absolutely to die for, Lenora. You'll have to teach me to make it."

"I'll be happy to, but I warn you—it doesn't always turn out this well. It all depends on the quality of the shrimp."

"And thanks for putting the seafood crepes on the menu. I've been craving them all week."

"Langston told me, and we have to keep our mom-to-be happy."

"Are there more biscuits in the warmer?"

"Yes, I'll get them," Lenora said.

"Let me," Matt said, already pushing back from the table.

Matt had promised that Shelly's first Collingsworth Sunday brunch would be a treat, but she hadn't been prepared for anything quite so elaborate or delicious. Nor had she expected to be so totally welcomed into the family. It wasn't that they'd made a production over having her join them at the massive dining room table. Quite the contrary.

Once the introductions had been made, they'd just accepted her as one of their family. Their large, boisterous, hungry family. The only surprise was Jeremiah. From all the talk she'd expected him to react negatively to her. Instead he'd given a sly wink as they'd bowed their heads for the blessing. Almost as if they were coconspirators in a private scam.

That had been the end of their bonding, though. Before the amen had cleared Langston's mouth, Jeremiah had dived into his meal with gusto. All else was forgotten for him. The rest of the family spent as much time chatting as eating.

Matt's sister Becky complained that her estranged husband wanted to keep the boys an extra week that summer. His unmarried sister Jaime raved over a dress she'd found on sale at the Galleria.

Langston's pregnant wife, Trish, described the newest addition to the nursery—a musical mobile of prancing horses that Langston's office staff had given them. Bart's wife Jaclyn, hung on Trish's every word. Shelly suspected she was eager to have a child of her own.

Shelly made herself the designated listener. It was her job. She reminded herself of that with every breath.

Just because the Collingsworths exuded bountiful love and warmth within their family circle didn't mean that they hadn't crossed the lines of morality and legality when it came to their business dealings.

Just because Matt could send desire zinging though her didn't mean he wasn't guilty of treacherous acts in the name of greed. Just because his kiss had haunted her dreams last night didn't mean she couldn't keep him at a distance and see this assignment through.

And why was she even thinking about him now?

She turned her attention to Melvin Rogers. He'd been introduced as a family friend, but she knew from the conversation that he worked for Langston. He was young, early thirties, Shelly guessed. His sandy-blond hair was cut stylishly short. He was nice-looking, but lacked that enigmatic cowboy appeal the Collingsworth men wore so well. He was more West Coast suave, though even that didn't quite ring true.

Too bad she wasn't sitting close enough to him to question him about his duties with Collingsworth Oil; that would have to wait for a more opportune time. Showing too much interest in the business at this point could work against her.

"Looks as if you're going to be in good hands, Jeremiah. I'd hire me a physical therapist just to improve the scenery around my place if I could get one as pretty as Shelly."

Billy Mack, the outspoken, slightly past middle-age man they'd introduced as a neighbor, made the statement. Eerily everyone grew quiet. The gazes moved from her to Jeremiah as if they were watching a tennis match.

"What the hell are you talking about? *Physical therapist.* I'm through with all that."

"I told you I'd hired a physical therapist," Lenora said. "I thought you realized that it was Shelly."

"And I told you I don't need some woman haranguing me about exercise. I'm too damn old for that. Now pass me the salsa so I can liven up these eggs." He banged his cane on the floor to emphasize his point. Derrick nudged his twin brother and they both snickered, appreciating that there was some excitement at the table.

Lenora wiped the corner of her mouth with her napkin. "I'm sorry, Shelly. But just ignore Jeremiah's outburst and enjoy your brunch. And don't worry. He'll come around. He just doesn't take to change very easily these days."

"I understand. I'll take it slow with him, give him time to get to know me and vice versa."

Thank God for Jeremiah. Thank god for any lifeline to keep her from totally drowning in the warm, loving dynamics of this family.

Right now, her real past was no longer her past. The mother who'd never had time to fit Shelly in between her constant stream of relationships was no longer her mother. Shelly had a new reality—one created for her by the agency.

Fake name, fake past, fake memories. Unfortunately, her emotions still belonged to her real past. Matt and his family were playing havoc with those.

The rest of the meal passed with no more outbursts from Jeremiah, and the adults, were lingering over coffee when Matt's cell phone rang. He excused himself to take the call and returned a few minutes later, all smiles.

"That was Ed Guerra," he said. "A cop from New Orleans recognized the shooter from the sketch that was sent out to all the law-enforcement personnel in Louisiana and Texas. The guy's got an arrest record thicker than a bound volume of all the Harry Potter novels, and he's been spending a lot of time in Houston of late."

"Like we need more criminals in Texas," Langston said. "Did the sheriff give you a name?"

"Frankie Dawson. He deals drugs and makes explosives. I'm not sure how the two go together, but the cop from New Orleans says he's got a reputation for planting bombs under the houses of people he considers his enemies."

"Sounds like a real charmer." Bart set his cup on the table. "Has there been an arrest?"

"No, but the sheriff is convinced this was a case of mistaken identity."

"What makes him so sure?"

"It's the guy's modis operandi. He has a temper and when someone crosses him, he goes after them. Usually it's about drugs, but not always."

A muscle tightened in Langston's jaw as he leaned over and put an arm around the back of his wife's chair. "Aidan deals with that sort of senseless violence all the time in the drug-infested areas of Houston, but I didn't think something like that could happen in Colts Run Cross."

"It's sick," Lenora said. "Shelly could have been killed by this thug. Any of us could have been, if we'd been in his path."

"Let's just hope he's arrested soon," Trish said, "and that he stays in jail."

Lenora placed her hands flat on the table and straightened her back as if taking a stand. "That settles it, Shelly. You did nothing to provoke the shooter and there's no reason for you not to move into Zack's old suite in the big house. Now who's got an argument with that?"

No one spoke up.

"You'll have privacy and the full run of the ranch," Lenora continued. "Unless you've changed your mind about wanting to live and work here. I wouldn't blame you if you have, but I'm hoping you'll stay."

"I wouldn't dream of running out on you before my job is done." Finally she could say something that was true.

AFTER THREE DAYS AND NIGHTS of living in the big house, surrounded by Collingsworths, Shelly felt as if she'd known them all her life. Odd as that may seem, since her life had been nothing like this.

They were relaxed and easy, yet never dull. Everyone was totally involved in their jobs or their passions—apparently even Matt. She'd only seen him once since he'd dropped off her and her luggage on Sunday night.

Shelly was certain he was still upset that she'd jerked away from his kiss. Not that she blamed him. And not that she could react differently, if she had it to do all over again. She was on solid ground now, fitting in with the family, chatting with whoever happened to be around. She could do nothing to jeopardize that progress.

The only first-week goal she hadn't accomplished was to gather some grain of information the agency could use. No luck there. But she had finally gotten Jeremiah to agree to *talking* to her about therapy. One small step toward her getting to keep both feet firmly planted inside the Collingsworth compound.

The sun was barely over the horizon, and the house was quiet except for the ticking of the grandfather clock in the downstairs hallway as she started down the staircase. She'd tossed and turned all night, never able to fall into a deep sleep and finally deciding to give it up and go for a brisk walk.

Her CIA phone vibrated in her pocket before she hit the bottom step. She hadn't talked to anyone in her office since she'd reported her status early Monday morning and a call this early in the morning could mean trouble. She ducked out the back door and took a worn path to a spreading oak tree near the riding arena. She climbed up and perched on top of the fence, locking her heels on the second rung before returning the call.

It was Brady who answered, and even though it was an hour later in D.C., she knew he seldom started work this early.

"Quick response," he said, always a man of few words. "Are you still on the ranch?"

"I am, but I'm outside and apparently am the only one stirring at this ungodly hour."

"Can't sleep, huh?"

"You got it," she answered, yawning into the words.

"How's it going?"

"Nothing to report. I've met all the family except the younger brother Zach who's honeymooning in Hawaii, but I'm not getting any guilty vibes and little talk of business."

"I told you they'd project a good image."

"It's a little more than that. They're patriotism seems to be a lot more than lip service. They talk about duty and honor openly. They don't just practice philanthropy, either. They live it."

"It can still be an act."

"Sure, but why go out of their way to impress a lowly physical therapist?"

"You make a good point. But they're filthy rich. They had to step on a few toes to get where they are. You stamp enough toes and cross enough lines, the morals issues get blurry. And you've seen the evidence we have on them. There's way too much smoke for there not be a raging fire somewhere."

"I concede that someone in the organization may be guilty, maybe even one of the Collingsworths, but not all of them. Take Becky Ridgely."

"That's the daughter married to the pro football player?"

"Right. She's a full-time mother with almost no connection to the business end of things. And there's Jaime. She works at the oil company, but only three days week. And she hadn't worked there long. And Matt's into ranching—not oil."

"It was his name that was found on an illegal alien a few nights ago."

"Anyone could have given the man Matt's name. Finding it on him doesn't automatically make Matt guilty."

"Doesn't make him innocent, either. That's the second time you've mentioned him. You're not falling for Matt Collingsworth, are you?"

"Of course not. I barely know him. I'm telling you my gut instincts. That's all I have to go on as yet. But I did meet someone I think you should check out."

"Who's that?"

"Melvin Rogers. He works with Langston Collingsworth at the oil company."

"Will do, but Ben hasn't mentioned him and Ben's getting in pretty tight with some of the management team. That gets me to the real reason I called. Ben thinks another large transfer of funds is about to occur."

Brady had the utmost faith in Ben and had been ecstatic when he'd landed a position inside the Houston office of Collingsworth Oil. Shelly saw him as an arrogant blowhard, but then so were more than a few of their most successful agents.

"Is this speculation or does Ben have proof?"

"He intercepted correspondence from a foreign bank verifying that they are ready to make the requested transfer at a moment's notice. The money will be paid in cash to someone in Saudi Arabia who was identified only by a series of numbers."

A one-time code name that would be almost impossible to trace. Her stomach rolled sickeningly, the fact that the news bothered her made her sicker yet. Why couldn't she fully accept that at least one of the Collingsworths was likely padding the pocketbooks of some of the world's most evil men?

"Keep your eyes and ears open every second, Shelly. There's not a lot of time to work your way into their confidence before this goes down. Don't miss an opportunity to get close and personal with any of the family members. If we get the chance to turn this into an arrest, we'll want every scrap of evidence we can lay our hands on."

"Right."

"Keep me posted."

"You, too, sir."

"Busy day. Gotta cut and run."

And he did. She dropped the compact-shaped phone back in the velvet pouch with her lipstick and pushed it deep into the front pocket of her jeans. As long no one saw her talking on it, it was doubtful anyone would take it for a phone.

"Hi, there."

She jumped at the sound of Matt's voice. She hadn't heard him approach. She'd have to be more careful in the future, keep a closer vigil when she was on the phone with head-quarters. She took a deep breath to still her nerves.

"Good morning, Matt."

"How's the arm?"

"Pain's gone, except for a twinge every now and then, when I bump it or move it the wrong way."

"Good, and how's it going with my teddy bear of a grandpa?"

"Not as well, but we're meeting after lunch to *talk* about the possibility of his giving me and my methods a try."

"That's progress."

"You're up and out early, or is this the typical ranching starting hour?"

"Actually I've been up most of the night. One of our mares foaled during the wee hours of the morning and there were complications."

"Is everything okay?"

"Both mother and baby are doing fine. The equine vet just left. I don't have to call him often, but this birth had me worried."

"It must be a valuable horse if you had to miss sleep yourself with all the wranglers you have."

"It's not a matter of monetary value. I'm the rancher.

When there's trouble with my animals, I take responsibility. I like it that way and think it's probably why I never got into the oil business. Nursing cold, black crude doesn't offer the same type of gratification as watching a calf or foal take that first wobbly step."

Shelly studied Matt in the soft glimmer of the sun's early-morning rays. She could see fatigue in the slight stoop to his shoulders and in the wrinkles at the corners of his gunmetal gray eyes. Mostly she saw his strength. Taut muscles. Sun-bronzed skin. Tough as steel, yet caring enough to be there for a horse in need of care.

He'd be a fantastic lover.

The thought ambushed her, then took over her senses so fast, it left her reeling. Vivid images pressed into her mind. His arms around her, his hands and fingers imprinting into her back, his legs tangling with hers.

"Would you like to see the new foal?"

"Yes," she answered quickly, thankful that if he'd noticed her flushed state, he hadn't mentioned it.

He put a hand on the small of her back and walked beside her until they'd cleared the stable doors and entered the soft filtered light inside.

He spoke to the horses as they made their way to the rear of the building, calling each by name and stopping occasionally to scratch a nose poked in his direction.

"You're good with them," she said.

"Not nearly as good as my sister-in-law Kali, but I like to think I connect with them."

"So you're not just a cowman?"

"I'm a man of many talents."

There was no mistaking the sensual teasing tone of the comment. So maybe he had noticed how flustered she'd become and sensed it had to do with him.

"There he is," Matt said. "Sakima."

"He's so little."

"Probably didn't feel that tiny to his mother when she was pushing him out."

"Is Sakima an Indian word?"

"Yes, it means king, or so I've heard. I don't know which tribe the word stems from, though."

"Sakima, I like it. And it fits him. He already looks regal."

"Lying in the hay by his mother's feet?"

"Well, he's just a prince now."

She leaned against the door of the stall as Matt checked out the newborn. The mother stared at him nonchalantly as if she knew her baby was in good hands.

Shelly felt as if she'd entered another world, galaxies removed from the world where she normally lived on the vicious edge between crime and punishment.

The sun was higher in the sky when they left the stable and the heat dug in between her shoulder blades and stroked her cheeks. She didn't see how a person could ever get used to South Texas summers. "I should get back to the house and let you get to work," she said.

"Yeah." But he didn't turn to walk away. And neither did she.

"I hope you're not still upset with me about the other night."

"I thought you were upset with me."

"No. I was wrong," he said. "It won't happen again. Scout's honor. The next time we kiss—if there is a next time—you'll have to ask for it."

If he didn't move his hand and step away soon, she'd start begging now. But only because her mind refused to believe he could be guilty of aiding the enemy. She couldn't possibly have this kind of attraction for someone who would fund cruel, heartless killers.

"C'mon," he said. "I'll walk you back to the house. Juanita's likely got coffee brewed and breakfast cooking by now."

Matt wanted her to go with him. He'd made that clear, but he wouldn't want her around for a second if he realized she was here to help rip his family apart and send one or more of them to prison.

She'd wanted this assignment so badly she'd practically begged for it. Now she wished anyone was here but her. Still, she'd do her job. This was a battle the good guys had to win.

AS MATT HAD SUSPECTED, Juanita was already busy in the kitchen when he and Shelly made it back to the big house. He and his brothers had a hell of a time talking his mom into hiring a cook. But she'd quit complaining and started singing Juanita's praises long ago.

Shelly had taken her coffee back to her room instead of having it with him. Just as well. Matt had too much to do before the morning got away from him; he couldn't dawdle over breakfast. He'd grabbed coffee and a hot tortilla that Juanita had stuffed with bacon, eggs and a dash of salsa before heading out.

He was pumped, though after the night he'd had he should be dragging. He had been before he'd spotted Shelly—with her cute little bottom perched on top of the fence.

Running into her had affected him like a double shot of espresso. Every part of him had come instantly to life—especially parts that had no business springing into action with a woman who'd pulled away from his kiss the other night.

The kiss was his mistake, but he hadn't had a woman get to him like this since his first year in college when Betty Estes had taught him the kind of tricks he'd never learned in Boy

Scouts. Then, it had been mostly physical. Hell, it had probably been all physical, but at eighteen, what else was there?

He wasn't eighteen now. He was pushing thirty-four, had dated lots of women, made love to his share and had managed to walk away from all of them without losing a night's sleep. He wasn't proud of the fact that he never became emotionally involved. It was just the way it was— or the way it had been up until last Friday.

He hadn't had a decent night's sleep since he'd met Shelly, and his appetite was none too great, either. Worse part was that she wouldn't clear out of his mind. He'd try to think of feed production; she'd dance all over the numbers. Even last night, when he should have had nothing but foaling on his mind, he'd thought about how close she'd come to losing her life.

She got to him on a dozen different levels and in ways he hadn't began to comprehend. Part of it was probably the whole woman-in-jeopardy scenario. He felt compelled to protect her, whether she wanted to be protected or not. Her mix of vulnerability and spunk was a more powerful aphrodisiac than any perfume on the market.

Not that Shelly didn't smell great. Normally he was pretty much desensitized to odors. A steady dose of manure and cow droppings could do that for you. But Shelly smelled like spring. Fresh. Clean.

And he was letting this get out of hand. Shelly was temporary. He barely knew her. And he didn't have time for a lot of mushy relationship business.

Still, there was something about her. And regardless of what the sheriff had said, he couldn't quite push past the suspicion that she might still be in danger. Reason enough to keep his eye on her for a while even if she didn't seem to want his company.

"IT WAS A SIMPLE TASK. YOU screwed up. And you know how I feel about mistakes."

"The random violence angle was your idea. I carried it off just like you said. The car has more holes in it than a rapper's jeans. There's no way she should have walked away from it alive."

"Alive? She's barely hurt. I want her dead. Now."

"She's just a friggin' physical therapist. What's so important about knocking her off?"

"That's not your concern. I give the orders. You take them. It's called 'money rules.' You have one week, or the deal is off."

Sweat pooled under his armpits and dampened the front of his shirt in spite of the fact that the air conditioner in his Houston apartment was clunking along at full power. He needed that money. He could clear out of the country with it, leave his enemies behind and live like a king in Mexico on what he'd get for this job. But a week...

"I need more time. She's living at Jack's Bluff. I can't just storm the place and take her out. They have security and gun-wielding wranglers everywhere."

"One week. Work fast. You're not the only one whose time is running out."

Chapter Nine

Jeremiah hobbled into the first-floor study exactly twenty-two minutes past their scheduled meeting time. She knew he had neither forgotten the appointment nor become confused about the meeting time. She'd found him in the front yard talking to Billy Mack about five minutes before they were supposed to meet and reminded him.

He swung his cane as he sat down, banging it against the leg of a bookcase before propping it against his chair. "A pretty young woman like you ought to have better things to do with her time than waste it talking to an old codger like me."

"I'm getting paid for my time and I certainly hope it won't be a waste."

"You could have saved yourself a trip to Texas if my daughter-in-law wasn't always trying to do my thinking for me. I may not get around like a young whippersnapper, but I'm not senile."

"Glad to hear that," Shelly said. "I don't treat senility, but I'm a very competent physical therapist. I'm pretty sure I can help you—if you're willing to put forth some effort."

Jeremiah checked his watch as if he had another appointment, then frowned as if he were late for it. "I'm over a year post-stroke and not stupid. I know the odds of seeing any kind of improvement at this point are slim to none."

"Actually, recent research has proved that certain exercises used routinely can lead to substantial improvements in balance and range of motion." Fortunately, she'd done her homework. "I can show you articles on that if you'd like."

"Keep your articles." He picked up his cane and pointed it toward the window. "You see that big oak tree out there?"

She nodded, wondering where he was going with this.

"I planted it the year my only child was born."

He had to be talking about Lenora's late husband. That would make the tree approximately six decades old. She'd known that Randolph was the only heir to the Collingsworth fortune before he'd fathered his own large brood.

"I built this house, too," Jeremiah continued, "with my own hands and little help from anyone else."

"You did a great job. It's still in marvelous shape." She still had no idea what point he was trying to make, or if he had one.

"I made Collingsworth Oil what it is today, too."

Now, they might be getting somewhere.

Jeremiah scratched a pale, wrinkled cheek, then nudged his brass-rimmed glasses up the thin bridge of his nose. "Sure my son improved the bottom line. So has Langston, but I set the wheels in motion. I made deals they'd never think of, took risks they'd never dare."

His mouth started to twitch and he stared into space, finally letting a smile reach his lips. At first she thought he'd lost his train of thought—a not so uncommon trait for men his age even if they haven't suffered a stroke—but when he spoke again, she knew he was merely reliving a time when he'd felt far more potent than he did today.

The smile disappeared and his expression became drawn.

"I was worth something to my family back then. Now I'm just a liability. And my huffing and sweating and taking on a hundred more aches in these worn-out joints just so they can feel like they tried to rehabilitate me isn't going to change the fact that I'm old. So take your theories and your exercises and go back to Atlanta."

In spite of his bluster, he was clearly depressed over the changes since the stroke and quite likely afraid of failure if he went back into therapy. He had probably never shown weakness nor felt this powerless in his life.

Her heart went out to him. She wished that it didn't. Sympathizing with him made trying to wheedle information so much more difficult. But she had no choice, especially now that she knew his mental functioning was more stable than first impressions had suggested.

He'd been CEO of Collingsworth Enterprises until the stroke, and knowing what she did of his personality, she suspected he'd run things the way he saw fit, whether or not Langston agreed. Admittedly, he took risks and made deals they wouldn't have considered.

Yet he was out of the office and apparently uninvolved with company operations and the money continued to exchange hands—and at an escalated rate.

Jeremiah leaned forward, using his cane for support. "Go home, or stay here on the ranch if you like. It doesn't make two cents' worth of difference to me. Just don't badger me about therapy. It's not going to happen."

"It's your call," she said. There was no reason to antagonize him, when her purpose was to get close. "I'd love to hear more about your work with Collingsworth Enterprises, though. Big deals. Risk taking. It sounds as if you've had an exciting life."

He studied her, likely judging whether or not she was

serious or merely humoring him. He must have decided in her favor, since he leaned back in his chair and let go of the cane.

"The oil business is not what people think it is. Those complainers always screaming about the price of gasoline don't know the half of what we go through to keep their big cars running."

"They should probably talk to you," she said.

"Dart tootin' they should. It's not the *Beverly Hillbillies,* you know. You don't just walk out in your backyard and find oil. You gotta spend money and go hunting for it."

"You must have to make deals with all kinds of people."

He nodded. "Especially today. The world's changing. The balance of power is steadily shifting." His hands knotted into bony fists and his voice rose. "And now we got the CIA breathing down our neck." He was practically screaming now. "The CIA doesn't have jack squat—"

"What's going on here?"

The interruption startled Shelly. She looked up to see Matt's brother Bart standing in the doorway—his eyes narrowed, yet piercing.

He glared at Jeremiah. "What's the problem?"

"I'm educating Shelly about the oil business," Jeremiah said.

"I'm sure Shelly's not interested in the inner workings of the company. Besides, you know our rule. What goes on at Collingsworth Oil stays at Collingsworth Oil."

"I thought that was Vegas," Shelly joked, trying to ease the tension that had walked in with Bart. No such luck.

"Is the therapy session over?" Bart asked.

"Never got started," Jeremiah said. "Never going to."

"In that case, how about taking a ride over to Tom Greer's with me. He's cutting his operations back since his wife was hurt in that car wreck in February, and he's got some hay-baling equipment he wants to sell."

"Since when do you want my opinion on equipment?"

"I don't. I'd just like your company and you and Tom always find things to talk about."

Shelly didn't buy it. What he wanted was to keep Jeremiah from saying more about the CIA. It was just her luck that Bart would show up at that precise moment. Her would-be patient had been in the mood to talk. She'd see that she found time alone with Jeremiah again, hopefully before the day was over.

Jeremiah departed with Bart, leaving her to ponder a half dozen possibilities she couldn't back up with facts. Maybe Jeremiah had been the one to initially secure oil deals by contributing to terrorist causes. But who had taken over where he left off? Langston? Lenora? Or was it as Brady believed—an accepted practice of Collingsworth Enterprises with multiple family members savvy and going along with the practice?

But then Brady only knew the family by reputation. He hadn't eaten with them, slept in their houses. Hadn't kissed Matt Collingsworth.

Her lips tingled at the memory, followed by a crush of longing that swept through every inch of her. She gathered her resolve.

This case was far too important, and if she stepped down from the case, there was no way the agency could just slide another agent into her spot; she was the only agent who was a licensed physical therapist.

Yet the memory of the kiss clung to her lips and her mind as if she'd been bewitched.

THE BIG HOUSE WAS exceptionally quiet for the rest of the afternoon. Lenora and Jaime were at their jobs in downtown

Houston. Becky had taken her young sons and the two boisterous lab puppies—one of which belonged to the honeymooning couple—to visit friends at a neighboring ranch.
Matt was nowhere to be seen, and even Juanita had finished
dinner preparations and gone back to her own house for a
few hours downtime.

Apparently her schedule was flexible. She showed up in
the mornings, put breakfast on the table and stayed busy in
the kitchen all morning. Lunch was on the table at twelve and
eaten by whoever showed up. The participants varied, but
usually included Becky and her sons, a wrangler named Joe
Bob who was practically family and totally charming, and
sometimes Bart and Jaclyn.

Shelly had shown up every day, hoping to glean some
tidbit of useful information. That had been a bust, though
she'd loved talking to Bart's wife, Jaclyn, and found her
open and interesting.

Becky was more difficult to relate to. She was friendly,
but nowhere near as outgoing as her younger sister Jaime.
She never talked about herself or her estranged husband.
The boys, however, talked about their dad almost constantly.
It was clear they missed him and couldn't wait for their
summer visit with him in July.

Shelly picked up one of the family albums from the book-
shelf in the family room and dropped to the sofa to peruse
the snapshots. She skimmed the first few pages, mostly
images of a much younger Lenora and a very handsome man
who must have been her late husband, Randolph. These must
have been taken right after their marriage—or before. Lenora
didn't appear to be much past her teens when the pictures
were taken.

Shelly turned the next page and a loose snapshot slipped
from the folds and fell into her lap. There was writing on the

back and Shelly checked that out even before looking at the photo.

I love you more than life itself, Randolph Collingsworth, and I can't wait to marry you and bear your children. Your world will be my world. Hugs and a million kisses, Lenora.

Lenora had been so young, yet she'd followed her heart. It had worked for her. She was one of the lucky ones.

Shelly's mother had fared much worse. She'd chosen the wrong man—over and over again. A half dozen stepfathers and more "uncles" than Shelly cared to remember had taken up residence in their house. Shelly had even liked a few of them. No matter. None ever stayed for long.

Restless now and haunted by memories she preferred to leave cloaked in shadows, Shelly retuned the album to the shelf and walked toward the back door, swinging through it for a reviving breath of fresh air.

She'd made it to the bottom step before an uneasy feeling sent a shiver up her spine. Apprehension and training cued her senses, and she scanned the area looking for movement and listening for any errant sounds. A slight breeze rustled the leaves in the nearby oak trees and ruffled her short hair. A crow cawed. Another answered.

Nothing amiss, but the flesh around her freshly dressed wound prickled, a reminder of the bullets that had fallen all around her mere days ago.

A car engine sounded in the distance, coming steadily nearer. A shaky breath burst from her lungs. She wouldn't be alone much longer. The relief that accompanied that thought both surprised and disturbed her. Even temporary timidity in a CIA agent was unacceptable.

The car pulled up in the driveway and Jaime jumped out as soon as the engine died. She waved to Shelly, while a tall man dressed in cowboy attire climbed from the passenger seat. Shelly recognized him instantly as the young cowboy who'd been staring at her in Cutter's Bar the other night.

Jaime hung on his arm as they crossed the drive and joined Shelly at the back door. "This is Leland Adams," she said, draping herself over his shoulder and holding on to his arm as if he might try to escape. "Leland, meet Shelly, my grandfather's new physical therapist."

He showed no signs of recognizing her and she decided it was best not to point out that he'd been casually flirting with her in the bar.

"Leland's new in town," Jaime said.

So he had likely been looking for a woman to hook up with the other night. She wasn't sure how Jaime had connected with him so quickly, but she could have met him before then or else last night when she'd gone out with friends.

A lonesome cowboy would notice Jaime at once. She was what the hip magazines would classify as a super hottie. Great looks, a sparkling personality and dressed to entice.

"I'm going to give Leland a quick tour of the house and then we're driving out to the lake to catch dinner and a sunset—if there's one to catch. The weather forecast predicted a line of thunderstorms heading this way."

Shelly glanced out the window. There was no sign of rain, but she knew from her research that Houston weather was unpredictable, something about the nearness to the Gulf of Mexico.

"Tell Mom I'll be home early, since I have to work tomorrow." Jaime accompanied the word *work* with a gagging expression.

"Spoken like a true heiress," Leland said.

Obviously he was not so new to these parts that he didn't know of her family's wealth. But then the Collingsworth name ranked right up there with the Bush name in Texas prominence.

Leland was the stranger. Shelly considered warning Jaime to be careful, but she didn't want to come across like an alarmist. In all likelihood, Leland was just a cute cowboy out for a good time.

"Sounds like a fun evening," Shelly said. "But you'd best take good care of her, Leland. I'd hate to have her four brothers take you to task." If Leland was even half smart, that should be enough to keep him from trying anything with Jaime she didn't want.

He grinned and raked his fingers through his scraggly hair. "I'll be a perfect gentleman."

It struck Shelly again how odd it was for her to feel protective of a member of the family she was investigating on extremely serious charges.

But, thus far, nothing about this assignment was textbook. Her goal was to blend into the family so seamlessly that they forgot she was around and talked freely in front of her. She'd expected that to require major effort on her part. Instead, the effort was in not becoming so much a part of the family that she couldn't see them objectively.

Leland stopped and turned as he started to follow Jaime up the stairs. Shelly felt his stare boring into her just as she had the other night at Cutter's Bar. A second later, he looked away and took the stairs two at a time, easily catching up with Jaime before she reached the landing. He must have whispered something funny to her as he did, because their laughter echoed through the house.

Restless, Shelly exited via the back door and strode off at a brisk pace. She was almost at the stable before she realized she'd unconsciously gone in that direction. The image of Matt flashed into her thoughts, his hair mussed and his chin whiskered from the sleepless night he'd spent bringing a reluctant colt into the world.

Her knees seemed to liquefy as the image solidified and seared its way into every corner of her mind. Just hormones, she told herself, and her body's way of protesting the fact that it had been denied physical satisfaction for so long.

Forcing her feet to keep going, she pushed through the door of the stable. Afternoon sun poured through the high windows, painting bright stripes of gold across the walls and the few horses that remained in their stalls. A cinnamon-colored steed whinnied and stuck his head over the stall door as if entreating her to pay him a visit or take him for a ride.

She stopped at his stall and hesitantly reached to scratch his nose the way she'd seen Matt do it this morning. He balked and backed away, pawing at the straw and sending it flying beneath his firm belly. Shelly jerked her hand away and backed up so fast she stumbled against the opposite stall.

So she was jittery around horses. Big deal. She faced killers, didn't she?

The stable door squeaked open. She steadied her breath and turned to see Matt and Bart step inside, their bodies haloed in a bright beam of sunlight.

"Langston can handle it," Matt said.

"He's been saying that for months, but the CIA shows no sign of letting this go."

Shelly shrunk against the wall, thankful the rays of sun fell to the right of her, leaving her in the shadows. Hands at her side, she stood perfectly still, hoping the steed wouldn't give her away. Miraculously, the horse ignored her, his head turned as if he, too, was eavesdropping on the conversation.

"They don't have anything," Matt said. "If they did, they'd be making arrests, not rattling cages."

Shelly's heart slammed hard against her chest. Did this mean Matt was in on the payoffs?

Bart knocked away a spider that had dropped from the ceiling on a silky thread and landed right in front of his nose. "The feds wouldn't be spending this much time on the investigation, if this wasn't more than a fishing trip."

"Langston says it's under control," Matt reiterated. "And he's too shrewd a businessman to be leaving anything to chance."

"He's got a pregnant wife ready to deliver within the month. That's his focus right now."

"Can't blame him for that."

"I'm not blaming. I'm just concerned, that's all. We can't afford…"

The steed picked that moment to shake his head and snort loudly, drowning the last of Bart's sentence. The men swung their attention in her direction. Shelly gave up the shadows and stepped into the middle of the aisle that separated the rows of stalls, waving and smiling as if she hadn't heard a word of their conversation.

Matt started toward her. "Couldn't stay away from Sakima, could you?"

"Not a chance. He's so adorable."

"I didn't see you standing there," Bart said. "Why didn't you say something when we came in?"

"You were having a conversation. I didn't want to interrupt."

"Conversation's over," Matt said. "Let's check out the new foal."

"You two go ahead," Bart said. "I'll come back later with Jaclyn. She loves the young colts and I've promised her a sunset ride anyway—if the rain holds off."

Matt chatted casually as he checked out the newborn and

the mother—talking as much to the horses as to her. His tone was calming, and the bond between him and the animals couldn't have been more evident if it had been tangible.

She was as mesmerized by him as she was of the mare and colt. But instead of putting her at ease, his presence created currents of crackling electricity that zinged through her senses.

He finished with the horses and walked back to where she was standing. He trailed a finger down the length of her arm, and the innocuous touch felt like fire on her skin. Finally she looked up. His face was inches from hers, his lips taunting her, daring her not to remember how they'd felt pressed against hers.

"Let's go for a ride."

"A horseback ride?" Her voice was breathy, her heartbeat erratic.

"Why not? There's plenty of time before dinner, and I promise I'll fix you up with the gentlest mare on the ranch. We can take the wooded trails. It will give you a chance to see some of the undeveloped land you can't get to by car."

She and Matt—alone in the woods, with this wild hunger for him raging inside her. Did she dare risk it? Was he fighting the same insane passion, or was all the heat and sensual tension radiating from her?

Not that it mattered. Some agents had no doubt used sex to weaken a suspect's resistance. She couldn't. Nor could she put her own heart on the line when there was no chance this could work. She had little faith in love under the best of circumstances. This was the worst.

Even if Matt was as innocent as she wanted so desperately to believe, he'd hate her once he'd found out she'd tricked her way onto Jack's Bluff Ranch for the express purpose of bringing his family down.

"It's okay to say no, if you don't want to go ride with me," he said.

"No, I'd like to go horseback riding," she said, forcing herself to do the job she'd come to do. "As long as we take it slow. Remember, I'm a city slicker."

"We'll go as slowly as you like, and I'll be right by your side. I'll go saddle up a couple of horses and meet you outside the stable in about ten minutes."

She managed a nod, waiting until he was out of sight to fall back against one of the support columns that separated the stalls. For the last few years, she'd feared she'd never fall into anything that even resembled love again.

What a time to find out she'd been wrong!

"LANGSTON, THIS IS BART. Do you have a minute?"

"Yeah, I'm just finishing up here at the office and about to leave for home."

"Are thinks okay with Trish?"

"Perfect. She went to her gynecologist this afternoon. He thinks it will be a couple more weeks before she goes into labor. She's antsy, but feeling good. What's up with you?"

"Shelly Lane."

"What about her? Mom says she's a perfect fit for the family and she's confident Jeremiah will warm up to her in no time."

"I know. The rest of the family has no qualms at all with her. Even Jaclyn is fond of her."

"But not you?"

"She worries me."

"Anything specific?"

"I walked in on her and Jeremiah this afternoon and she had him talking about the oil company's problems with the CIA. Then this afternoon, Matt and I ran into her in the stables. She had to have heard and seen us but she didn't say a word until we spotted her."

"C'mon, you surely don't think she's a spy for the CIA?"

"It's possible. What's more likely is that she's trying to get something on us that she can use in a blackmail scheme. She wouldn't be the first to try some kind of scam to get money out of the family."

"You're getting a little paranoid. She's here because Mom hired her."

"I just don't want any trouble. We already have enough."

"Are you suggesting we try to pressure Mom into firing her?"

"No. But I think you should make sure the private investigator leaves no alley unexplored where her background's concerned."

"I'll see that he gets that message. And thanks for the heads-up though I'm surprised to be hearing this from you. Matt's usually the suspicious brother."

"Not this time. He lit up like neon when he noticed her in the horse barn. I think he's finally met a woman who fires his engine."

"And you want to get rid of her. Mom would die if she knew that."

They both laughed, but Bart was certain Langston would follow up with the private investigator. Only now, he was almost sorry he'd said anything.

Matt liked her. That should have been good enough for Bart.

MATT STOOD BESIDE THE TWO saddled horses, their reins in one of his hands. He reached the other out to Shelly. She quivered as she took it, her nerves on edge and not just from the size of the horses.

Her CIA phone vibrated. She ignored it. Brady would have to wait. It was time to ride.

Chapter Ten

The two horses walked side by side along the swiftly running creek. It was swollen from the May rains, but would likely be bone dry by the end of August.

Normally, Matt would have soaked up the scenery, noticed every new growth of underbrush, checked for deer tracks to see if the herd numbers were up or down, and enjoyed the scurry of squirrels and the plodding of the turtles along the muddy banks.

All he could see today was Shelly.

She'd monopolized his thoughts from the moment he'd met her, though he'd tried to convince himself it was caution that had sent him back to town to check on her that first night. That had been a crock, a protective facade he'd pulled over his eyes to keep from acknowledging the way she got to him.

The timing for this couldn't be worse. This was his busiest time on the ranch. He had a million things he should be focusing on. Langston was worried that the troubles with the CIA were coming to a head, and anything that affected any member of the Collingsworth family affected them all.

It had always been that way, especially between him and his brothers. They might fight with each other, but go against one of them and you went against them all.

Even worse than the timing issues, Shelly was the wrong woman. The ranch was his life. She was a city girl, here on a Texas adventure. But the day-to-day reality of ranch life didn't provide the kind of excitement most women envisioned when they thought about cowboys.

He wasn't all that exciting, either, and he was smart enough to know it. He might have the money to live the life of the rich and famous, but he had no desire to jet set or to be a staple of the *Houston Chronicle*'s society section. Ranching was his life.

"I never thought I'd say it about a horse ride, but that wasn't half bad," Shelly said, "except when I spotted that snake wiggling its way through the pine straw."

"A king snake. They're harmless." The rattler she hadn't seen wasn't, but there was no need to point that out when he was drowning in the most seductive smile he'd ever seen.

Bad timing. Wrong woman. So why the hell did just being near her get his blood and juices pumping this way?

"Are there snakes in the creek?"

"It's Texas. Snakes are everywhere."

"Not inside the big house?"

"No, only the brave would take on two rambunctious boys and Jaime."

"That is not true, Matt Collingsworth and you know it. You adore your nephews and Jaime is—"

"Jaime is Jaime. We'll leave it at that."

"I like her. I like the whole family."

"Even Jeremiah?"

"He's growing on me. I think at least some of the bluster comes from his being afraid of all the changes that happened so quickly. Growing old slowly is bad enough, but when a stroke steals so much from you in the blink of an eye, it's difficult to adjust."

"I know. He's a pretty terrific guy when you think about it. He had to be father to all of us after my dad died. He had that drill-sergeant personality even then, teaching us about honor and responsibility.

"I can still hear his lectures ringing in my ears. 'A man is only as good as his word.' That was a favorite line of his. I probably heard that at least once a day growing up. It worked, though. I *am* as good as my word."

"And did your brothers buy into his philosophy?"

"Yeah. I'd have to say they did. We're all very different, but if one of my brothers tells you something, you can be sure it's damn straight. What about you? Do you have brothers? Sisters?"

"No. I'm an only child."

"Spoiled, I guess."

"Rotten."

"That explains that strange smell."

She stuck her tongue out at him. The kidding backfired; he imagined her tongue tangling with his own. He'd vowed that if they kissed again, she'd have to ask for it. Who'd known that promise would be so difficult to keep?

Still, it was probably for the best. Fat chance he'd ever be satisfied with just a kiss, when desire was bucking around inside him like a mad bull.

Shelly looked upward. The wind caught her hair and blew wispy strands of it into her face. His hands itched to reach across the distance between them and tuck it behind her ears. His fingertips would brush her cheeks, might even trail to the curve of her neck. His mouth went dry.

"I think I felt a raindrop," she said.

He pulled his attention to the weather long enough to check the sky. He'd meant to keep an eye on it, but his attention had been captured by more exciting things. A raindrop plopped on his nose, followed by a few more, though the moisture was barely a mist at this point.

"Main storm's to the west of us and moving that way," he said. "We won't get the brunt of it, but it's probably best to go to my place and wait it out. It's nearby."

The words had spilled out of his mouth so fast, he had to wonder if the idea hadn't been skirting the edges of his subconscious before he said them, maybe the reason he'd brought her in this direction.

Moisture glistened on the cleft of Shelly's breasts, just above her blue cotton T-shirt. The tightening in his groins was almost painful. His apprehension level surged.

"Or we can just start back to the big house," he offered. "We'll get wet, but nothing that a few towels and a change of clothes can't remedy." And nothing would happen there that either of them might regret.

She hesitated, but only for a moment. "Your place."

He'd almost swear there was a hint of anticipation in the tone. More likely, he was reading into it what he wanted to hear. But he'd keep his promise. The first move would have to be hers.

THE RAIN WAS STILL FALLING steadily when they reached Matt's rustic home on the edge of the woods. It dripped from Shelly's hair, the cool wetness meandering down her forehead and the back of her neck.

Matt climbed off his horse first, and then walked over to give her a hand dismounting. She slid her feet from the stirrups and he caught her at the waist, pulling her from the saddle and into the circle of his arms.

Matt's hands tightened around her waist, his thumbs digging into her flesh, searing through her shirt. The air 'ween them grew steamy, and she was aware of the quick intake of his breath when his gaze fixed on the distinct outline of her pebbled nipples thrusting against the wet shirt.

His thumbs inched higher burying into the soft mound of flesh and pushing her breasts upward. She had a crazy urge to lift the shirt, raise it over her arms and fling it into the rain. Instead she crossed her arms over her chest.

"I'll secure the horses out back," he said, releasing her suddenly and pulling away. "The door's unlocked. Make yourself at home."

She raced to the porch as a streak of jagged lightning lit the gray sky. The rain might last longer than they'd thought—minutes or hours that she'd be alone with Matt, stranded inside his cozy cottage with electrical currents firing between them that were far more dangerous than the storm.

Get close was the name of the game, she reminded herself, but not so close that disentangling herself would jeopardize her mission—or shatter her heart.

Once inside, she slipped out of her shoes and padded to the bathroom for a couple of towels. She used one to dry her dripping hair and face and took the other to the back door for Matt.

She was dabbing at the back of her neck when she heard the stomp of his boots just outside the door. "Tell me I can't pick great weather for a ride," he teased as he swung the door open and joined her inside.

He pulled off his hat and placed it on a shelf near the back door with a couple of other western hats, all well-worn. Locks of his thick hair fell over his forehead. Impulsively, she reached to push them back then caught herself and pulled her hands back to her side.

A smile touched his wet lips, and though he didn't say anything, she knew he realized what she'd done and knew exactly why she'd pulled her hand away. His knowing she was fighting her feelings, like a young woman afraid of losing her virginity to a virile cowboy, made this all the worse.

She tossed him the dry towel.

"Thanks." He blotted his face, but never took his eyes off her. "I like the view," he said, grinning and for the first time openly flirting with her, "but you might want to get out of those wet clothes."

The ridiculous blush crept to her flesh again. "A good idea. Do you have a shirt I can borrow?"

"Better than that. I have a robe. I'll put your wet clothes in the dryer."

Getting out of the wet clothes made perfect sense, but the thought of being naked beneath a robe that had hugged Matt's body and likely even retained the soapy, musky scent of him was risky at best.

But Matt didn't wait for an answer. He disappeared down the hall and returned a minute later with a cotton robe still encased in plastic.

"You don't have to give me a new one."

"It's the only one I have," he said, placing it in her hands. "A Christmas gift from Becky who thinks I lack the rudiments of civilized living out here."

"Christmas was months ago."

"The Christmas I received that was years ago. A man living alone doesn't have much use to be covered up when he gets out of the shower."

Another image she didn't need. She took the robe and whispered a hurried thanks before she returned to the bathroom. Locking the door behind her, she leaned against it a few seconds, regrouping and taking deep breaths to still the sensual turmoil.

No man had ever affected her the way Matt did, and she

was still mystified as to exactly what it was about him that got to her. His virility? His rugged good looks? The way his mouth had felt on hers? Or was it the way he'd taken over as her protector from the moment they met?

Probably all that and more, and still she had to let it lie. She had a job to do and she'd do it. It was the way it had to be. She only prayed that all her instincts were right and that Matt was as innocent as she believed him to be. If she was wrong about that, she may as well turn in her resignation today.

The snap on her wet jeans was difficult to maneuver and by the time she'd undone it and the equally reticent zipper, she felt a little more in control. Pushing them past her hips, she let them fall to the floor and then kicked them past her feet.

Unfortunately, the uneasiness returned when she slipped her fingers beneath the elastic waist of her panties. Some of her friends back in D.C. routinely went without underwear. Shelly never did, and the realization that she was about to be doing just that in Matt's house sent heated spikes from her brain right to the core of her being.

She hesitated, then wiggled her panties over her hips and kicked them off. After all, the robe was not transparent. Determinedly, she yanked the wet shirt over her head and reached behind to unclasp her bra. The straps slid over her shoulders and arms and she let the lacy garment fall to the floor with the rest of the wet clothes.

Grabbing the robe, she ripped off the plastic and shook the garment loose. She shoved her arms into the sleeves and pulled it tight. It hung from her shoulders like a sheet, touching her almost nowhere except the shoulders. She yanked on the ties, bunching the fabric at the waist.

Her mirror image taunted her. Very attractive. Kind of like

a pregnant rag doll. That should take care of any sexual urges Matt might have. She gathered her wet clothes, realizing as she balled the panties and bra that there was no way she was handing them to him.

He'd said to make herself at home. Surely that included using the dryer without his supervision. She found the laundry room just off the garage. It was as neat and clean as the rest of the house. Apparently Matt did not like clutter. Yet another trait she could live with.

Live with. Her insides rocked insanely. How had that thought crossed her mind? At best she was here to ruin his family's reputation. At worst—well she didn't even want to go there.

She threw the clothes into the dryer and went to find Matt. He was in the kitchen, but unfortunately he hadn't been nearly as accommodating in his choice of attire. His dry jeans rode low on the waist. His clean, white western shirt was open with the tail of it hanging loose. The spattering of dark hairs on his chest seemed to be inviting her fingers to curl around them.

His bare feet slapped against the tile floor as he stepped toward her. "Cocktail hour. The choices for fancy drinks are limited, but I have the basics on hand. Scotch, whiskey, gin and tequila. I can fix you a margarita if you like, or there's wine. I'm not much of a connoisseur, but Jaime stocks the wine closet at home and she makes sure I have few choice bottles on hand."

"Right, so you don't embarrass yourself with lady visitors."

"I could probably count them on one hand. Haven't we already had this conversation?"

"You said you'd never come close to getting married. We didn't discuss numbers." And she had no business doing it now. But the question was out there, and she had no inclination to call it back.

"Then we should probably set the matter straight." Matt set two highball glasses on the counter and turned to face her. "I date, Shelly, actually more than I want, since my mother has decided I need a wife. I don't have sex indiscriminately, and I haven't had unprotected sex since my last semi-long-term relationship. That was two years ago."

"I didn't mean to give you the third degree."

"It's okay. I like things out in the open. I told you, I'm an uncomplicated kind of guy."

"What are you having?" She neatly changed the subject.

"Vodka and tonic."

"I'll have that, too. Easy on the vodka."

"Afraid I'll get you drunk and have my way with you?"

"That might complicate your life."

"It just might."

When the drinks were ready, they returned to the den, with its floor-to-ceiling windows that looked out on the pond and the forested area to the right. Raindrops danced on the windows intermingling with late afternoon shadows. Shelly settled in the upholstered chair nearest the window and pulled her bare feet into the chair with her, tucking them under the robe.

Matt took the sofa. "What made you become a physical therapist?"

Answers to any questions about her background had all been scripted and rehearsed. They were nothing near the truth. Oddly, she'd like to speak honestly with Matt. But she couldn't tell him about how she'd been perfectly happy as a physical therapist until 9/11 had made her rethink her career goals. She'd watched the towers fall on television and knew then that she had to do something more for her country. The CIA had been her choice.

Instead, she went to the memorized script. "The mother of one of my best high school friends was a physical therapist. She loved her work and just hearing her talk about it made me want to give it a try. And it got my dad off my case to become an attorney like him. After reading John Grisham's books, I *knew* I didn't want to be a lawyer. Too many slimy clients."

"I can understand that. Do your parents live in Atlanta?"

"They did. Dad retired last year and they moved to Florida. They live on what I only half-jokingly refer to as reservation for retired people. They call it paradise."

"I plan to retire right here. Well, actually I don't plan to retire at all. Hopefully, I'll stay busy until they bury me beneath Jack's Bluff earth." He swirled his drink in the glass. "Most people spend a lifetime looking for their niche. I was born into mine."

"Seems all you're missing is someone special to share it with." A stupid thing to say, especially when she knew that life as he knew it was likely to disintegrate in days—maybe hours. Yet she found herself waiting for his reply, as if it mattered more than anything she could have asked.

"If I found the right person, I'd marry her in a heartbeat."

"But you haven't found her yet?" The husky vibration in her voice gave too much away. Echoed the emotions riding much too close to the surface, emotions she shouldn't be having.

"I didn't say that. I'm not sure how I'd know, unless the woman I was attracted to reciprocated a little. Maybe by not turning away every time the heat and passion started to build between us."

His attraction for her was on the table now, heady, more intoxicating than the drink. A hunger shot threw her, raw and so fervent it hurt. She ached to cross the room and fit herself into his arms. Longed to feel her body pressed against his, to hear his heart beating in time with hers.

Instead, she struggled with a response.

She was so lost in the moment that she didn't hear the approaching car until she saw Matt's gaze dart to the window. She followed suit in time to see Sheriff Guerra step out of his squad car.

Matt opened the door while the sheriff was still stamping up the steps. "What brings you out in the rain?"

"I was looking for Shelly Lane. She wasn't at the big house, so I thought I'd try your place."

"Lucky guess." Matt tilted his head in her direction.

A knowing smile crossed the sheriff's face as he looked from her to Matt and back to her again.

"We were horseback riding and got caught in the rain," Matt said. "Shelly's clothes are in the dryer."

His smile widened. "Darn rain can sure mess up a good afternoon."

Matt ignored the comment. "Do you have news for Shelly?"

"Yep. A couple of state troopers found Frankie Dawson this morning up near Lufkin."

Her shooter. Shelly stood and tried in vain to smooth the bunched fabric. "Did they make an arrest?"

"Little late for that. He was slouched over the steering wheel of a stolen sedan with two bullets in his brain. Likely never lived long enough to know what hit him."

"A gang-related hit?"

"More'n likely. Violence begets violence. The rule of the streets. But I guess we can close your case. Just thought you'd like to know that you don't have to worry about him anymore."

"Thanks."

"Would have been nicer to have answers," Matt said. "We still don't know for certain that Shelly was a random victim."

"And now you probably never will, but it sure looks that way to me. Guess I'll get back to town. Can I give you a ride back to the house, Shelly, or do you want to wait out the rain?"

She hesitated. Surprisingly, Matt didn't. He was already buttoning his shirt and he looked all business now. "How about giving both of us a ride to the big house? That way I can pick up my truck. I'll get Jim Bob to trailer the horses back."

Confusion clouded her mind and chilled her heart. She was falling hard for the protective cowboy. She had to call Brady and tell him she couldn't do this any longer. Time and opportunity were running out.

BILLY MACK CLIMBED THE steps to the front porch of the Collingsworth house and sauntered over to the swing where Lenora nursed a tall glass of iced tea. "You were awful late getting home tonight."

Lenora planted her feet and stilled the swing so that her neighbor could sink down beside her. "Were you watching for me?"

"Yep. Can't have my widow-lady neighbor coming in at all hours. People will talk."

"Only if you go gossiping to them," she teased. "Besides, it's only ten past seven." Billy Mack had been her neighbor since the day she married Randolph and moved to Jack's Bluff. She and his wife had been best friends, crying and laughing together as they raised their kids.

Now it was she and Billy Mack who were left. He spent increasingly more time hanging around her ranch, even flirted occasionally. She didn't mind. He was lonesome. But both of them knew her heart would never belong to anyone but Randolph.

"Did you see a dozen fender benders?" Billy Mack asked.

"At least. You'd think Houstonites would be used to rain, but the concept of slowing down for wet streets never seems to catch on."

"Does the rain have you down, Lenora, or is that CIA business still playing havoc with your spirits?"

"Men are supposed to get less attentive to women's feelings as they grow older. How is it nothing gets past you?"

"You're not that difficult to read. When you're happy as a hog in a mud hole, you're smiling. When your face is long enough to eat oats out of a butter churn, you got something troublesome on your mind."

"I am troubled," she admitted. "Mostly for Langston. He's taking the brunt of the CIA investigation when he should be concentrating on nothing but the birth of his son."

"So they haven't given up with those absurd allegations?"

"No, and they're beyond absurd. Langston runs a tight ship and he would never do anything traitorous. He's loves his country and he's moral and upright. They should be able to see that, but they don't."

"Is Melvin still in charge of getting to the bottom of the charges that company money's gone to terrorist leaders?"

"Yes, and he says all the business dealings have been squeaky clean."

Billy Mack spread his hands on his thighs, letting his blunt, weathered fingers stretch along the denim of his worn overalls. "Maybe Langston should hire someone outside the company to take on that task."

"Who would know more about the operations than Melvin? He's Langston's right-hand man."

"It's just a thought," Billy Mack said. "I know you all think of him as family, but he's not, you know."

Lenora stopped the swing again, shifting so she could look Billy Mack in the eye. "What's that supposed to mean?"

"What I said. He's just not family. That's all."

"He's *almost* family. And Langston has hired an outside accounting firm to go over the most minute detail of every money exchange made over the past year. He expects to get that report back soon."

"Good. I always knew that boy had something in his head besides nits."

They both looked up as a car came down the side road and turned in the drive. Ed Guerra waved from behind the wheel, but didn't get out. Matt and Shelly did and were joined quickly by two excited black lab puppies.

Shelly stopped and scooped Chideaux up in her arms. That one belonged to Zach's wife Kali, but was staying with them while Zach and Kali were on their honeymoon. Blackie belonged to David and Derrick and much preferred to run and bark than be held. He was busily circling Matt's heels now.

"What was the sheriff doing out here?" Lenora asked as Matt and Shelly joined them.

Matt squatted on the top step and tangled with Blackie while he filled them in on the details about Frankie Dawson's murder.

"I hate to hear any of this," Lenora said. "It's a sorry welcome to Texas we've given you, Shelly."

Shelly nuzzled Chideaux beneath her chin. "It wasn't your fault. We have crime in Atlanta, too."

"I still hate that you were hit with the worst of our great state as soon as you arrived. But I just had an idea. I've coerced Matt into going with me to the black-tie art auction for Children's Hospital Saturday night. Why don't you join us? It will be fun."

Shelly turned to Matt, but Chideaux had joined Blackie in the game of tussle and Matt kept his attention focused on the dogs.

"Tell her you want her to join us," Lenora encouraged.

Matt still didn't look up. "It's up to her."

Matt's hardheadedness could be annoying at times, and Shelly was such a nice lady.

"I really don't have anything to wear," Shelly said.

"You and Jaime are practically the same size, and she has a closet full of formals. I'm sure you could find one you like, and I know she'd be glad for you to borrow a dress."

"I wouldn't want to impose…"

"Nonsense. I'll talk to Jaime when she comes in."

"Which reminds me, I'm supposed to tell you she went to dinner with a friend and will be late," Shelly said.

"If she's too late tonight, you can pick out a dress tomorrow."

"Okay, Mrs. Collingsworth, if Jaime doesn't mind and we find one that fits, count me in."

Still no comment from Matt. Lenora was starting to get tired of throwing perfectly suitable women at him only to have him ignore them. Actually, they probably weren't all perfectly suitable, but she didn't see what he could possibly have against getting to know Shelly better. She was not only pretty, but personable and smart.

Shelly excused herself and went inside.

"It wouldn't hurt you to be a bit more attentive when there's a gorgeous woman around, Matt Collingsworth."

Matt smiled, kissed her on the cheek and took the steps two at a time. "Good night, Cupid, er, Mom."

"You should listen to me," she called after him.

"I think you can let up with the matchmaking," Billy Mack said as Matt drove off in his own truck.

"I just want Matt to be happy and to find someone to share his life with the way his brothers have. You know how important that is, Billy Mack. We lost our loves too soon, but imagine if we'd never had them."

"Don't even want to try." He reached over and lay his hand on top of hers. "But I'd say Matt's got some powerful heart-bustin' feelings for Shelly bucking around inside him right now."

"Do you really think so?"

"Sure as shooting. Open your eyes. You'll see it."

Lenora let the comment sink it. She wasn't certain Billy Mack was right this time, but he frequently was. And after all, she'd had a good feeling about Matt and Shelly from the first time she'd met the new physical therapist in that hospital room.

"Don't go cooking up plans," Billy Mack said. "They're adults. They'll take care of things on their own."

Easy for him to say, but she knew Matt. He'd need a push. Luckily, a plan was already forming in her mind. She couldn't do a thing about the CIA, but this she could manage.

Chapter Eleven

Trish squirmed beside Langston in the king-size bed. He reached over and spread his hand on her swollen belly and felt the solid kicks. His son was growing inside the woman he loved.

He'd heard the word joy used all his life. Now he knew what it meant—a heart so full that it sometimes felt like it might rise like a helium balloon and float to the heavens. His might have done just that were it not for the problems with the CIA weighing it down.

Trish thrashed in her sleep then jerked and started inching away from him. He watched her in the silver of the moonlight streaming through the window. She was always beautiful—always would be in his eyes—but he literally couldn't keep his eyes off her since she'd become pregnant. He'd missed this with his daughter. He wanted to treasure every second of the beginnings of his son's life.

"Little fellow keeping you awake?" he asked

"I think he's playing football with my kidneys." She eased her legs over the side of the bed. "I've got to go to the bathroom again."

"Can I get you something? Warm milk? Cheese crackers and fudge?"

"You're never going to let me live that down, are you?"

"Probably not."

During the first trimester she'd had this unreasonable craving for cheese crackers and fudge. The first time it had hit had been in San Francisco where she'd gone with him to a conference. He'd left their hotel room at two in the morning to go in search of the snack.

Crazy thing was, he hadn't minded at all. If she'd decided she needed a couple of stars and a planet or two to go with it, he'd have done his best to get that for her, too.

When she came back to bed, he made a place for her in his arms.

"I'm sorry I woke you," she said. "Maybe I should start sleeping in the guest room until the baby's born."

He buried his face in the soft flesh where her neck met her shoulder. "Does that mean the honeymoon's over?"

"It means the breadwinner needs his rest."

"You didn't wake me," he admitted. "I was as restless as you."

"It's the CIA investigation, isn't it?"

"Yeah."

"You know their allegations are false, Langston. If they had evidence, they'd be prosecuting. You've said that yourself a hundred times over the last few months. They don't have evidence—because there isn't any."

"I may have been overly optimistic." He felt her tense and wished he didn't have to tell her this, not now with the baby due so soon. He'd been fretting about it all night, and had finally acknowledged that the truth would be the only way he could break the worst of the news to her.

"Is there something I don't know?"

"I told you I'd hired an accounting firm to analyze our financial expenditures to the minutest detail."

"And there's no reason to think they'll discover anything your own accountants haven't."

He pulled her closer. "Only they did. Over six million dollars that was allocated to purchase equipment from overseas suppliers over the past two years has vanished. The equipment was reportedly delivered, but in actuality was never even ordered. There is no paper trail for where that money actually went."

"So you think it might have gone to a terrorist organization?"

"I don't know where in the hell it went, but I plan to find out." Here came the really hard part. "I'm going to have to make a trip to our Middle East facilities, Trish."

"When?"

"I have reservations for a Tuesday flight."

"But the baby is due within the next two weeks."

"I hope to be back in a week."

"But what if the baby's early? You wouldn't be here. Oh, Langston, you can't miss the delivery. You've talked of being there and seeing your son take his first breath since the moment I told you I was pregnant."

"I know." But better to miss the first breath than miss his son's whole life while he sat in a prison cell. "I think Collingsworth Oil has been set up, Trish. I don't know why or by whom, but someone—or some group—has orchestrated a brilliant plan to put us under and send me—and possibly other members of the family—to prison. I can't let that happen."

"You can't take this on yourself. Every member of the family is an equal owner of Collingsworth Enterprises."

"The oil business is my baby. I'll let them know what's going on, but I have to take full responsibility for this."

"But you'll be able to straighten this out. I mean, there is no chance they can arrest you, is there?"

"No, of course not," he lied.

"I'm afraid, Langston."

"Don't be, sweetheart." He was afraid enough for both of them.

IT WAS AFTER TEN BEFORE Shelly had an opportunity to return Brady's call. Her suite, a spacious bedroom and cozy sitting room, had formerly been Zach's quarters. The only other room in this wing was the game-and-billiards area and it was empty now.

She didn't know if her supervisor would answer or have the call transferred to someone working night shift at headquarters. Brady answered on the first ring.

"State your name and business."

Her pulse quickened. Shifting to this high level of security could not be good. "It's Shelly," she said, adding her private code word though she knew he'd recognize her voice. "Are their new developments in the Collingsworth investigation?"

"The money is expected to be transferred on Monday. We've got it covered. There's a good chance Langston Collingsworth will be under arrest by Monday evening. He's being followed now in case he tries to leave the country. Arrest of other family members will likely follow shortly, with CEO Lenora Collingsworth second in line."

The walls of the room started closing in on Shelly, and she held to the back of the loveseat to keep from sinking to the floor. "Are you certain the Collingsworths are actually behind this?"

"Everything looks that way. Langston Collingsworth is the one name that's stayed constant as we've progressed up the evidence level. But the names of all his brothers are playing prominently in the latest deal."

Her head begin to spin. There had to be a mistake. "I'm

inside the family situation," she said. "I find it virtually impossible to believe M—" She stopped herself. "I can't believe anyone in the family is guilty."

"They've been misleading people for a long time, Shelly. Playing their good-old-boy rancher and philanthropy cards without a miscue. It sounds as if they may have even gotten to you."

"No." At least she didn't think so. She was almost certain she hadn't been misled. If she was right… Her mind changed gears and was off and running in another direction. "The evidence could have been planted. This could be a setup."

"Not likely, considering that the investigation has been going on for over a year."

"But you do admit it's possible."

"The person setting them up would have to have a lot of power in the company. And motivation."

Still it was possible. "What do you want me to do now?"

"Stay on the assignment. I'll pull you off just before we make the arrest. In the meantime, don't miss any opportunity to gather information. Get back to me immediately with anything that could possibly affect our actions."

"I can do that."

"And, Shelly, be careful."

She could do that, too. She wasn't sure that she would. Now more than ever, she needed any scrap of info she could glean. And she'd go to any extreme to get it.

She was convinced that Matt wasn't involved in this in any way, but suppose she was wrong. Suppose her attraction to Matt had colored her every thought since she'd met him. Suppose he and all his brothers were GAS, guilty as sin. She sank to the loveseat, her mind a foggy blur of fears and possibilities. She couldn't pull out now, not with things racing toward culmination.

A light knock at the door jerked her to attention. "I'm coming." Her voice sounded as if it were being muffled by gauze. She took deep breaths as she crossed the room and opened the door to find Jaime dancing to a song she was plugged into via headphone.

"Oh, good. You're still up. I was afraid I might wake you." She pulled off the headphones. "Mom said you needed a dress to wear to a black-tie gala Saturday night."

"If you're sure you don't mind my raiding your closet."

"Not only do I not mind, I have several slinky, seductive numbers in mind."

"Not too slinky."

"There's no such thing."

"I'll need a sleeve to cover my bandage."

"Or a glittery stole. I have several. Come on back to my room. We'll play dress up."

Shelly wasn't up to playing anything, but she didn't dare turn down an opportunity to pick up a tidbit of new information. No matter what she believed—or wanted to believe—they were almost down to the wire and anything she learned could be valuable.

"Your date ended early," Shelly said as she and Jaime headed to Jaime's room.

"Leland is a dud. He's one of those jerks who just wants to hook up with someone with money. I run into more of those than I can count. Always have. It's the worst part of being from a rich family. The best part, of course, is the dresses. Wait until you get a look inside my closet."

"How did you figure him out so quickly?"

"All the questions. Like how big the ranch was, how much we were worth, that sort of thing. He even asked about you."

"What about me?"

"Who you were, what you were doing here and why. That

sort of thing. Like I said he was on the money make. He would have likely called you if he thought you were loaded. He still might."

"Hopefully not. I can see why dealing with guys like him would be a pain, but growing up rich must have had some advantages."

"Are you kidding? I didn't have a clue we were rich when I was young. My allowance wasn't even as big as some of the other girls in the class. Not only that, but I also had to work for mine, plus give some to the church.

"And believe me, there was no designer-label anything back then. As far as Mom is concerned, quality is not determined by price tag." Jaime mimicked her mother with that last phrase.

"She seems extremely generous now."

"She's generous to a fault, but she's also a stickler for responsibility. Which explains why she's unhappy that I haven't found my niche in life and settled down with a man or a career yet."

"You're working at Collingsworth Oil."

"Hopefully not for long and only to get her off my back. I've tried the corporate life. It's not me."

"I always thought big business might be interesting. Do you get to hobnob with the movers and shakers when you're in the office?"

"Yes, but that's not all it's cracked up to be. The movers and shakers don't have great moves. Give me a cowboy any day."

Shelly could definitely identify with that, though she wouldn't have understood it mere days ago. Jaime bounded ahead of her and was already pulling ball gowns from a walk-in closet the size of most people's bedrooms when Shelly caught up.

Jaime held up a blue silk that looked like something a starlet might choose for the Academy Awards. "Try this one on. You'd have the guys falling out."

Shelly ran her fingers along the low-cut bodice. "The guys wouldn't be the only things falling out."

"I have two-sided tape to keep the puppies in."

Shelly looked down to her size 34D puppies and shook her head. "Let's go for something cut a bit higher."

"Party pooper." Jaime pulled out several more before she came up with an emerald-green silk dress that made Shelly's mouth water.

"Let me try that one on."

Jaime kept rummaging through the closet while Shelly slipped out of her clothes and into the dress that hugged her bodice, waist and hips before flaring a bit to the hem. There was still plenty of cleavage showing, but no danger of a wardrobe malfunction. The most daring element was the slit that revealed lots of thigh.

Jaime returned with a beaded wrap to accessorize the dress and hide her bandage. She draped it over the bedpost and stopped to stare at Shelly. "Wow! You look fantastic. That dress was made for you."

"I love it," Shelly admitted, "but the slit may be cut a tad too high."

"For church, maybe. Not for an artsy affair. And I have just the jewelry to go with it." Jaime went to a wall safe hidden behind what appeared to be an electrical box in the closet. In seconds, she'd opened it and produced a diamond-and-emerald pendant and a pair of dangling emerald earrings. The trio was probably worth more than a year's pay for Shelly.

Shelly shook her head. "They're beautiful, but much too expensive. I absolutely can't wear them."

"You have to." Jaime circled her neck with the pendant and fastened the clasp. "They look terrific with the dress and your eyes. Just look at you. You'll have Matt panting so hard he won't be able to drive."

The mention of Matt brought the full weight of the investigation crashing down on Shelly again. The dress started to bind like ropes and she had to fight the urge to rip it from her body and run from the room.

"Shoes," Jaime said, oblivious to the change in Shelly. "What size do you wear?"

"Seven, but I can wear something I have."

"Not unless you have the perfect pair. I can't let you mess up that gorgeous dress with anything less. Becky's a size seven and she has a gorgeous pair of silver sandals I talked her into buying at the last Neiman Marcus sale. I doubt she's even worn them yet."

"I can't ask her to—"

"I'll do it for you, but she won't mind if you wear them. We share everything but men in this family. I'll even share that. You can have Leland."

"Now you're being much too generous."

A half hour later, her arms laden with her attire for Saturday night, Shelly dragged herself back to the guest suite.

With all her heart, she hoped Brady was wrong about the Collingsworths' guilt. But was he right about her? Had her feelings for Matt and her bonding with the rest of the family made it impossible for her to see the bigger picture? Or were the Collingsworths truly the most amazing and close-knit family she'd ever been around?

All she knew right now was that she'd never felt as if she belonged anywhere the way she felt here on Jack's Bluff Ranch. She knew it was only an illusion, one that could never last. Matt might be enthralled with her now, but he'd tire of her soon enough. Men moved on when relationships grew stale.

Shelly had witnessed that over and over again, with friends as well as her mom, though her mother held the I've-been-dumped prize. Not to mention that Matt would hate her when the full truth came out.

She opened her door and dropped the beautiful emerald dress on the bed. She'd wear it for Matt two nights from now. And then if things went according to Brady's educated predictions, she'd be on the team that sealed the deal against Matt's family.

There was no surer way to nip a relationship in the bud.

"FINE. I'LL FIND ANOTHER driver, but don't come whining to me the next time you're looking for a job you old reprobate."

Shelly had just poured her third cup of coffee of the morning when she heard Jeremiah's loud and very angry voice. She turned to the see him hobbling down the staircase, dressed in a suit and tie instead of his usual chinos and cotton shirt. His cane was in one hand, his cell phone in the other. Not the safest way for a man with his lack of balance to descend, but also not the time to point that out, unless she wanted to chance the cane flying in her direction.

"Can't get decent help anymore. Dadgummed idiots leave you high and dry without a never-you-mind about it," he sputtered to himself. He stopped when he noticed Shelly staring at him. "No, I'm not doing any exercises this morning," he snarled, taking the stairs even faster. "I got business to take care of."

"So that's why you're looking so dapper this morning."

He straightened his tie with a bony hand and stretched his thin, corded neck. "I have to go into town. That damned

CIA—paid for with my tax dollars by the way—has got nothing better to do than torment God-fearing, patriotic Americans."

"Are you meeting with the CIA?" Brady hadn't mentioned that.

"I plan to set them straight, as soon as I find out exactly what the Sam Hill's going on." He reached the bottom step and lifted his cane to point it in her direction. "They've got my grandsons buffaloed, but they don't scare me."

"Does that mean you're going into the office today?"

"I don't see any other way to get to the bottom of this."

A rather drastic move on his part; Lenora had told her he hadn't gone back since his stroke. Obviously, he had some mental grasp of the seriousness of the situation. She wondered if the rest of the family was fully clued in as well.

Sleep had been a long time in overtaking her troubled mind last night, and she'd had lots of time to rethink everything she'd seen and heard since first meeting Matt Collingsworth only a week ago. The crime and the family refused to meld in any scenario she concocted, leaving her more convinced than ever that they were being framed.

"Do you drive, Shirley?"

"It's Shelly." The stress was obviously affecting his short-term memory. "And I'm an excellent driver." Stunned that the opportunity to visit the height of the action might be about to fall in her hands, she wasn't about to blow it. "I'd be happy to drive you into Collingsworth Oil today, if you have a vehicle I can use."

"We can take my Lincoln. Not that I couldn't drive it myself if it came to that, but my license expired and I don't aim to have one of those smart-alecky Houston cops haranguing me."

"I'll drive. Give me fifteen minutes to change clothes."

"Make it ten."

"Yes, sir."

This would not only give her extended time alone with Jeremiah, but also give her a firsthand look at the business setting of the CIA investigation. She didn't know what she was looking for exactly, but it was imperative that she find it today!

THE EXECUTIVE OFFICES of Collingsworth Oil encompassed the eighteenth floor of an older and very stately skyscraper in downtown Houston. Shelly knew this from CIA research, but seeing it in person gave her a much better feel for the setup.

Her first impression was that Houston professional women were more sophisticated than she'd expected. After encountering two stylishly dressed young women in the elevator, Shelly was thankful she'd changed into the more chic of the two business suits she'd brought to Texas with her.

"I'll get that," Jeremiah said when she started to push though the double glass doors to the reception area.

She stood back and waited. He might be all brag and bluster when it came to conversation, but like the rest of the Collingsworth men, he was also a gentleman.

"Mr. Jeremiah," the receptionist called, obviously pleased to see him. "No one told me you were coming in." She rushed over and embraced him warmly.

"Don't go blubbery on me." His voice grew husky, and though the hug was quick and perfunctory, Shelly could tell his return after so long an absence had a bigger emotional impact on him than he would ever admit.

The receptionist turned her gaze to Shelly as if expecting some kind of introduction. Shelly extended her hand. "I'm Shelly Lane, Mr. Collingsworth's physical therapist and occasional driver."

"Nice to meet you." Her attention reverted back to Jeremiah. "Is Langston expecting you or are you here to see our illustrious CEO?"

"I'm here to see both of them. And, no, they're not expecting me."

"I'll let their secretaries know you're here."

"Don't bother. I'll announce myself."

"I'm not sure that's a good idea."

"Didn't ask you." His bluster was back. He started toward a closed door. "Come along, Shelly. You can wait in the lounge while I take care of business. The coffee's decent, or it used to be."

Shelly took a quick look around the reception area. The furnishings were in subdued earthy tones and rich woods and fabrics that embodied the family's ranching heritage.

Jeremiah looked straight ahead, his pace slow but steady. He didn't stop until they'd almost reached the end of the long hallway. "This is Langston's office," he said, stopping in front of a closed door. And that's my office." He nodded toward an open door just past them marked CEO, Lenora Collingsworth. "At least it was my office before this." He shook his cane as if it were the cause instead of the effect of his problem.

"It's nice you had Lenora to step in for you."

"It probably saved a lot of jockeying for power among my grandsons."

"But Bart and Matt don't seem that interested in the oil business."

"The CEO has final say at Collingsworth Enterprises. That's the oil company *and* the ranch. And while the boys are one for all when it comes to trouble, they don't like taking orders from each other."

"So Lenora basically took over to keep peace in the family."

"You could say that."

"I guess you must have given her a lot of help and advice."

"Nope. I wasn't doing a lot of helping with anything those first few months after the stroke. Luckily, my daughter-in-law didn't need much assistance. She just stepped in and took over. Made a lot of changes that probably needed to be made, though she tends to go overboard with handing out benefits."

"What kind of changes?" Shelly tried to sound only casually interested in the operations of the business.

"Better health benefits, more lenient family leave program. She's even got a fully-staffed nursery on the seventeenth floor so that new mothers can be close to their babies after they return to work."

"She's an amazing woman."

"Won't argue that, but they've got things in a hell of a mess without me."

"You mean because of the CIA investigation?"

He narrowed his eyes. "How'd you know about that?"

"You told me."

"Right. 'Course I did. I know that."

A slightly overweight middle-age woman with graying hair stepped out of Langston's office. Her pale gray suit was accented with a bright teal scarf that lit up her eyes. Her two-inch pumps looked expensive, but sensible. Her smile looked strained.

"It *is* you," she said, walking toward them. "I heard you were here and I had to see it for myself." She slipped an arm around Jeremiah's waist as if they were old friends. "You look terrific."

"Still a charming liar, I see." He turned to Shelly. "This is Langston's executive secretary, Lynette Hastings. And this is Shelly Lane." He stepped around them as they exchanged handshakes and moved toward the door she'd just exited. "Is Langston around?"

"He is, but he's about to start a very important meeting and I doubt he'll be free for a couple of hours."

"Did he tell you to say that?"

She was saved from answering by the arrival of Lenora. In lieu of a greeting, Jeremiah pointed his cane at her accusingly. "Why didn't you tell me there was a family meeting this morning?"

"I didn't want you to worry. How did you find out about it?"

"I was looking for Matt. Jim Bob said he and Bart had both gone into Houston for some kind of emergency meeting. I can still add two and two and come up with four."

The newly discovered possibility that Matt might appear at any moment upped Shelly's pulse, but only until the gravity of situation hit home again. Anxiety had pulled Lenora's usual smile into taut lines and painted dark circles under her eyes.

Lenora laid a hand on Jeremiah's forearm. "You're the rightful head of this family, and I should have told you about the meeting. Bart and Matt are already here. We should join them."

"Langston said Jeremiah should—"

Lenora put up her hand to interrupt Lynette. "It's okay. I'll handle Langston. Jeremiah's in this as deeply as the rest of us."

Shelly tried not to read too much into that last comment.

"You can wait in my office, Shelly," Lenora said, finally including her in the conversation. "It's more comfortable than the lounge. Martha can get you coffee and if you want something to eat, she can order it from the first-floor deli. Oh, and there are several daily newspapers on the bookcase behind my desk. Feel free to peruse them."

"Thanks."

That was Lenora. Hospitable, even when her heart was in anguish. Which would make them hate Shelly all the more when they found out she was an integral part of the team out to prove them guilty and end life as they knew it.

She sucked in a shaky breath as Jeremiah and Lenora entered Langston's reception area with Lynette close on their heels. If the evidence against the Collingsworths was false, there had to be a way to prove it.

If they were being framed, there had to be a way to prove that as well. It would have to be someone with decision-making power. Someone right here inside Collingsworth Oil. Perhaps someone sitting at a desk behind one of these closed doors. Someone with motivation to aid the terrorists or to destroy the Collingsworths. Maybe both.

The only flaw to that theory was that Ben Hartmann had been on the inside for almost six months now and according to Brady, was not picking up the same vibes that she was. Ben didn't have a sliver of a doubt that the current allegations were dead on.

In spite of Lenora's invitation to wait in her office, Shelly walked right past the open door and started back down the hall, checking the names on the offices as she went. Four vice presidents. She recognized all the names, though the only one of the four she'd actually met was Melvin Rogers. That was only because he'd shown up at the Collingsworth Sunday brunch.

She stopped outside Melvin's door. She'd love to snoop in his files, but even if he were in the big family conclave, his secretary would be in the outer office. She'd also love a chance to chat privately with Ben, but she didn't dare risk asking anyone where to find him.

A woman in a straight black skirt and tailored white blouse walked past with a tall man who appeared in his mid-thirties.

They were deep in conversation and barely noticed her as they passed. A second later, a gorgeous young woman who looked more like a super model than an oil-company employee stepped out of Melvin's office, pulling the door shut behind her.

His secretary? Good chance. Shelly hesitated only a second before she opened the door to Melvin's office and stepped inside.

As she'd hoped, the outer office was empty. Tense, her nerves on edge, she knocked lightly on the door past the secretary's neatly ordered desk.

She waited for Melvin's voice. When it didn't come, she turned the knob, pushed the door open and stepped inside. Leaving the door open a crack so that she could hear when the secretary returned, she crossed to the four large wooden file cabinets that were set along the side wall. She tried each one. The first three were locked. The fourth wasn't.

Without a clue as to what she was searching for, she opened the top drawer and scanned the files. Each was labeled with what appeared to be the name of a specific project.

Choosing one at random, she pulled a folder titled Drilling Project Twelve: Risk Analysis. There were pages of maps inside followed by various charts. A page slipped from the folder and she bent to pick it up.

At the sound of voices in the outer office, she shoved the file back in place and closed the cabinet door. The voices were louder now. She was almost certain that one belonged to Ben Hartmann, though she hadn't expected to run into him in the executive wing. The other might belong to Melvin.

A second later, the door opened. Definitely Melvin, looking as if he were about to strangle her or perhaps toss her from the window of the eighteenth floor. Ben looked downright shocked. Their gazes met and she could see the irritation burning in his eyes.

Melvin stepped toward her. "I'm sure there must be a very logical reason for your being in my private office, Miss Lane. For the life of me, I can't imagine what it could be. Care to set me straight?"

Chapter Twelve

Shelly tried to think of a clever comeback explanation to Melvin's rude insinuation. None came to mind, and Ben's glare wasn't helping. He needn't worry. She wasn't stupid enough to say or do anything to blow his cover or her own.

"I drove Jeremiah into the office this morning," she said, thinking fast. "I thought if you weren't busy, we might be able to grab a cup of coffee while I waited for him. Seems as if everyone else is in a meeting."

Melvin's eyes lost some of their fire.

"I guess I shouldn't have just walked in," she continued, "but Lenora told me to make myself at home around the offices, so I thought I'd give you a minute and see if you or your secretary returned."

Shelly was sure that wasn't exactly what Lenora had meant, but she could tell by the change in Melvin's expression that he was buying it. Vanity had him believing she'd like his company. She would, but not for the reasons he was thinking. Ben had moved over near the window and appeared to be studying the Houston skyline with avid interest.

Melvin leaned his backside against his desk. "How did you talk Jeremiah into coming into the office?"

"It was his idea. I just filled in when he couldn't readily find a driver."

"I'm sure he appreciated that. He gave up driving in Houston traffic several years ago, after losing a lane change battle with an SUV. I don't think Langston was expecting him today, though. Did he say why he wanted to come in?"

"Nothing that made sense."

Melvin nodded. "He's flirting with senility these days. That stroke did a number on him."

Ben stepped away from the window and toward the door. "You two seem to have things to talk about. Why don't I come back later? You can give me a call when you want to finish discussing that project?"

Melvin nodded. "Good plan. I'll take my lovely visitor to coffee and I'll get back with you before lunch. In the meantime, just keep what we were talking about under your hat."

"That's a given."

She'd interrupted Ben's opportunity for one-on-one time with one of the company's upper echelon. No wonder he'd looked irritated to see her. The phone on Melvin's desk jangled as Ben started to make his exit.

"My private line," Melvin said. "I'll need to take that."

"I'll wait in the hallway," Shelly offered.

Melvin motioned to them to close the door behind them as he took the call. Ben followed her past the secretary's desk, but grabbed her wrist before she reached the hallway.

"What the hell are you doing?" He mouthed the words. She had no trouble reading his lips.

"My job," she mouthed back.

He pulled a business card from his pocket and used a pen from the desk to scribble something on the back of it before pressing it into her hand. The secretary picked that exact minute to show up.

Shelly pocketed the card. Ben managed to unclench his mouth enough to smile at the woman and murmur good morning before striding away.

Melvin joined Shelly a few minutes later and suggested they take the elevator to the deli as the coffee was better there as was their chance of finding a table quiet enough where they could talk.

She blew off Ben's irritation. He was on the premises all the time. He'd had months to get close to Melvin. This might be her only opportunity to have a private chat with him, and it could be important.

Melvin knew the business. He also knew the family, was practically one of them. If he wanted, he could no doubt clue her in on any number of personal and business matters.

TEN MINUTES LATER, SITTING across from him at a table for two and sipping a latte, her optimism took a nosedive. So far, Melvin had failed to take any of the bait she'd offered. Most important, he'd avoided even her not-so-subtle attempts to steer the conversation to the CIA investigation.

She stirred another sprinkle of sweetener into her coffee. "How long have you been with Collingsworth Oil?"

"A few years."

"I'm impressed."

"By what?"

"You've moved up pretty high on the corporate ladder to have only been with the company a few years. So what's your secret to success? Wait, don't tell me. Let me guess. You're a Collingsworth relative?"

His eyes narrowed and he frowned as if she'd accused him of having bad breath. An odd reaction for someone who'd been accepted so fully into the business and the family circle.

"Rest assured, I'm *not* family."

"Judging from the way you fit in at brunch last week, they must think of you that way."

"I'm accepted, but I'm not to the manor born. There's always a difference. Not that I'm complaining. Just stating a fact."

But there was an edge to his voice. She wondered if he sensed the investigation was building to a crescendo. "What's it like working for Langston?" she asked, still hoping for some inside information to back up her theory.

"Probably calmer than working for Jeremiah. That is who you work for, isn't it?"

"I was hired by Lenora."

"That's interesting. I thought maybe Matt had hired you, seeing as how the two of you hit it off so quickly."

That felt a lot like a jab, though he was smiling when he said it. "Matt's been helpful," she said, resentful that he'd put her on the defensive. "But then, so has the rest of the family."

"I heard the man who shot you was murdered. Guess he didn't realize there are two rules around here that no one breaks."

"What would those be?"

"You don't mess with Texas and you don't cross the Collingsworths or their women."

She didn't like his insinuation that she belonged to Matt or the way he made it sound as if the Collingsworths had something to do with Frankie Dawson's murder. In fact, she didn't like Melvin, and she liked him less by the second. It was almost as if he knew she was with the CIA. But that was impossible. The only way he could know was if he'd heard it from Ben.

"Apparently the CIA doesn't know those rules, either," she said, deciding to take his remark and push it a bit further. "Jeremiah says they're investigating Collingsworth Oil."

Melvin propped his elbows on the table and leaned

closer, capturing her gaze with a penetrating stare. "You wouldn't be trying to squeeze information out of me, would you?"

"No. It's just that I find it extremely difficult to believe the Collingsworths guilty of anything the CIA would investigate. They seem so honest and forthright."

"I agree." He finished his coffee. "I hate to drink and run, but I've got to get back to work."

She took one last sip of her latte and then pushed back from the table. "Someone could be framing the Collingsworths." She threw it out as if the thought had just occurred to her.

"I guess anything's possible." He put a hand to the small of her back as they exited the deli. "But I wouldn't worry about that too much if I were you, Shelly. In fact, I wouldn't worry too much about anything."

"Why?"

"Life's too short."

There was no reason she had to ride up the elevator with Melvin, so she said goodbye at the deli and went to the restroom to read Ben's note. It, too, was short and to the point. *Back off. GAS.*

GAS. Guilty as sin. Meaning he must have obtained the conclusive evidence they'd been searching for. Maybe from Melvin?

She walked out of the building and crossed the street, stopping in the shade near the corner so the traffic would drown out her voice. Using her regular cell phone so as not to attract questioning stares, she put in a call to headquarters.

She needed facts, and she needed them now.

SHELLY HAD HOPED MATT MIGHT meet up with her and Jeremiah after the meeting and that they would ride back to the ranch together. Instead, Jeremiah had been waiting for her in Lenora's office. Apparently the family confabulation was ongoing; Jeremiah, however, seemed eager to go.

At his suggestion, they stopped for lunch at a small and very crowded Italian restaurant near the office.

The hostess, a middle-aged woman with a puffy eyes and overpermed hair, was all smiles when she saw him. "Mr. Collingsworth, I kept wondering when you'd be back to see us."

"I see you're still packing them in like sardines."

"Business is good." She glanced around the restaurant. "I'm afraid your usual table is not available, but I can still sit you in the side room." She turned to Shelly. "Mr. Collingsworth thinks Houston businessmen talk too loudly when they eat."

"What I said was, 'You need better acoustics,'" he reminded her. "Sounds like a school cafeteria in here."

"Very noisy," she agreed. "But nowhere else can you get my food. My mother's recipes. All fresh ingredients." She put a thumb and two fingers to her mouth to indicate it was delicious.

"Okay, quit your bragging and give us the quietest table you have."

"For two?"

"Of course, for two. Do you see anyone else?"

Jeremiah's abrupt manner didn't faze the hostess and apparent owner who just shook a finger at him. "You haven't changed a bit. I thought someone else might be joining you."

"Not today."

She led them through another door, and just as she'd promised, it was much quieter. There were no large groups of people, and since it was further from the kitchen, the banging and clattering was stifled. She offered them a table by the window. "Is this okay?"

"No, but we'll take it. Ought to get a free dessert since you gave my table away."

"Ought to charge you double for staying away so long."

She placed the menus on the table as he settled into his chair. "But in honor of your return, the drinks are on the house. The usual?"

He nodded. "With a double shot of scotch."

She turned to Shelly. "And for you?"

"Iced tea. I'm driving."

"You can take this back with you," Jeremiah said, handing the woman his menu. "I'll take the spaghetti and meatballs and a small Italian salad."

"Always your favorites," she said.

"I'll have the same," Shelly said, hoping she could manage enough appetite to force down a few bites. If she'd had more time with the Collingsworths before all this came to a head, she might have a better feel for the situation. As it was, she had only first impressions and her instincts to go on. Based on that, she could not accept the GAS verdict.

The drinks came quickly and the salads weren't far behind. Jeremiah tore into his as if forking lettuce were an Olympic event or at least a catharsis for his obvious frustration.

She let him finish most of his drink, hoping it would mellow him a bit, before approaching the subject of the morning's meeting. She ran her index finger along the side of her iced tea glass, collecting condensation. "Did the meeting at Collingsworth Oil ease your mind?"

He waited so long to answer that she wondered if he hadn't heard or had just decided to ignore her. Finally, he swung his leg around so that it was completely under the table and he was facing her. "It's more serious than I thought—the most ludicrous allegations I've ever heard!"

"Then the CIA really is targeting the company?" Her deceitfulness ground inside her like jagged glass.

"It's more like they're targeting the family, myself included. Even Lenora. They think we've been tossing money to terrorists in exchange for special favors on oil deals."

"What are they basing that on?"

"They claim they have evidence and that arrests are imminent. They're either bluffing or badly mistaken. My grandsons and my daughter-in-law wouldn't turn over one red cent to terrorists if their lives depended on it. The Collingsworth blood that runs through their veins would never let them." Anguish edged his voice and made his words shaky.

She'd never been more certain a man was telling the truth.

"That's enough talk of business," he said, when the waitress appeared with their overflowing plates.

She let the subject drop, though it was still claiming all of her attention. Evidence proved that money had gone from the accounts of Collingsworth Oil into the hands of the terrorists. If none of the Collingsworths were behind it, then someone else was. The options as she saw them were simple. Guilty. Or framed.

Ben Hartmann was convinced of the former. She was just as convinced of the latter, but there was zero evidence to back up her theory.

They ate in silence, until Jeremiah's plate was almost empty and she'd actually made a small dent in her serving.

Jeremiah dipped the end of a slice of garlic bread into his sauce. "Where were you when I was waiting for you in Lenora's office?"

"I ran into Melvin Rogers. We had a cup of coffee together in the deli."

He nodded but didn't comment.

"Your family seems very fond of him."

Jeremiah finished his sauce-soaked bread, but he was staring out the window now, almost as if he'd drifted to someplace else in his mind and forgotten she was there. When he finally spoke, his voice had a melancholy sadness about it that squeezed at her heart. "I'm glad she's not here to see this."

"Glad who's not here?"

"My wife. Corrine was a good woman. She had to be a saint to have put up with me. But then, she loved our son Randolph so much that nothing else ever mattered. Sometimes I think God called her home early just so she wouldn't have to face the heartbreak when Randolph's helicopter went down."

"How long has she been dead?"

"Almost thirty-two years now. She died with cancer right after Becky was born. Lenora said she held on long enough to hold her first granddaughter in her arms."

"You must have loved her very much."

"Still do."

Shelly tried to imagine that kind of love, a commitment that went years beyond the grave and still lived in his heart. "You were lucky to find each other."

"Damn lucky." He scratched his chin and then raked his fingers through his thinning hair. "Met her at a church social and I knew the minute she walked into the room that I was going to marry her. I felt like someone had hot-wired me and was sending enough current through me to light up the room. Sounds corny, but that's how it was."

The same way her insides grew hot and awareness zinged through her nerve endings when Matt was around. The way she melted at his touch and hungered to feel his lips on hers again. The way he monopolized her thoughts and had created that bittersweet ache in her heart.

"Have you ever been in love, Shelly?"

The answer stuck in her throat. Until she came to Colts Run Cross and Jack's Bluff Ranch, she hadn't even believed in love.

All she knew of relationships were the kind her mother had been in repeatedly. Four marriages. Four divorces. Countless failed affairs. And the liaison her mother was in right now was already on the downward spiral. Not that she and her mother talked often.

Jeremiah propped his elbows on the table and buried his head in his hands for long seconds before looking up and meeting her gaze. "If you ever love someone, Shelly, don't ever betray them."

"Betrayal must be difficult to forgive," she offered, thinking of how many times her mother had been betrayed, most of all by Shelly's father who'd simply disappeared when he'd found out she was pregnant; he'd never come back into their lives. His betrayal had haunted Shelly most of her life—until she'd finally hardened her heart against it and moved on.

"I don't know how difficult it is to forgive someone else, but it's dang near impossible to forgive yourself."

He'd been there. She saw in the heartrending depths of his eyes. He'd betrayed Corrine at some point and then she'd died and left him to live with the loss, and the pain of what he'd done. She reached across the table and laid her hands on his. He jerked his away as if the touch confirmed his vulnerability.

Betrayal was a death sentence to a relationship. No matter how felt about Matt, there was nowhere for them to go. She was undercover CIA—in his home and in his life under false pretenses. He'd taken her under his wing and offered protection.

Her job was to destroy him and his family.

There was no greater betrayal than that.

THE ENTIRE FAMILY, except for Zach and his new wife, were on hand for Friday night family dinner at the big house. Shelly had been amazed that the mood at the table barely reflected the problems they were dealing with. Shelly knew that was due to a major effort by everyone involved not to pull the others down.

It was also helped by everyone's excitement over a phone call from Zach and Kali saying they had cut their honeymoon short by a few days and that they'd be home tomorrow. David and Derrick had been especially thrilled over the announcement, because they'd been promised surprises from the returning couple.

At eight years of age, the twins had no conception that there could be problems that the adults in their lives couldn't handle. Shelly was pretty sure that Langston's teenage daughter Gina was also unaware of what they were up against. His wife, Trish, however, was the one exception. Anxiety haunted her dark eyes.

"Whose turn is it to do cleanup chores?" Bart asked after they'd lingered over coffee and dessert until long past the time Lenora had told Juanita to take the rest of the night off.

"I'll take care of it," Shelly offered. No sacrifice on her part; she'd feel much more comfortable alone in the kitchen than sitting as the lone traitor in the midst of the family. She'd expected a phone call from Brady all afternoon telling her to make some reasonable excuse for leaving and to get the hell out of Dodge.

He hadn't called. Nor had she. Leaving would be the same as giving up, and she wasn't ready to do that. Her mind was still wrapped around the idea that someone was framing them. But who had the capacity to do it and who hated them that much? And why? Without motivation, she had no argument to take to Brady.

"I'll help," Jaime said.

Matt stood from his seat at the opposite end of the table from Shelly and Jaime and started gathering the tableware. "What, no date on a Friday night?"

"As a matter of fact, I *don't* have a date tonight."

"Why didn't someone tell me the world was coming to an end?" Bart teased, then grimaced, as he no doubt realized how close he'd come to a truth that had nothing to do with Jaime.

"But I have two dates tomorrow, if that eases your mind."

"Better rest up for that," Matt said. "I'll help Shelly with cleanup."

Shelly's heart beat erratically at the prospect of being alone with Matt. She'd struggled all through dinner to keep her eyes from locking with his, had been afraid that he'd see the desire burning inside her. Afraid that he'd realize how hard she was falling for him.

She wanted nothing more than to go back to his house with him tonight and throw herself into his arms. She hungered for his kiss. Ached to press her body against his, to explore all the planes and angles of his hard body.

She wanted to make love with him, wanted it so desperately that she could feel the molten juices of desire pooling in the core of her being. But she couldn't, as long as the lies about her identity stood between them.

Everyone helped clear the table, but then wandered away, leaving only Matt and Shelly and a need that crushed into her chest with such force she had to hold onto the counter for a few seconds to get her bearings.

"I'll rinse and load the dishwasher," she said, knowing she needed to get busy and stay that way every second they were together. "You can put the leftovers away."

"Is that your best offer?"

"Try *only* offer, cowboy."

"Then I guess I'd better grab it." He reached around her for the leftover peas. "You were brave to drive my grandfather into Houston today."

"It went well. We had lunch and he talked a bit. And I had coffee with Melvin while Jeremiah was in the meeting with you."

"How did that go?"

"A little strained."

"He's under the gun with the rest of us with this CIA business. But no reason to bother you with any of this. Did you find a dress to wear tomorrow night?"

"I did."

A very sexy and elegant dress that would make her feel like a princess instead of the rat she felt like now. She slid a plate under the faucet at a bad angle and water splashed onto the front of her shirt. A few drops made it all the way to her face.

Matt picked up a dishtowel and blotted the drops from her cheek. Their gazes met for a second and her heart started beating so loudly she was certain he must hear it.

The towel dropped from his fingers and he slid both hands behind her head, his thumbs trailing her earlobes. "I'm trying to keep my promise," he whispered, his tone teasing though his voice was hoarse with emotion. "But I'm going crazy waiting on you to ask for a kiss."

That made two of them.

"Ouuu! Mushy stuff," David squealed as he rushed to the counter and grabbed a peanut-butter cookie from the few left on the serving plate.

"Kissy, kissy," Derrick chimed in, running right behind him to grab the last of the treats, followed by Blackie who merely barked his disapproval.

Shelly sucked in a shaky breath and leaned away from Matt to put the plate into the dishwasher. One more second and she might have been in Matt's arms, in spite of her good intentions.

She couldn't keep flirting with temptation and expect nothing to happen. Yet she couldn't leave as long as there was a chance she could clear him and his family. Damned if she did. More damned if she didn't.

Bart joined them in the kitchen just as she placed the last spoon on the dishwasher rack. He'd come to refill his coffee mug, but since the pot was empty, he decided on a beer. He offered them both one as well. Shelly took hers and escaped out the back door for a long walk, leaving the brothers to discuss whatever was on their minds.

Leaving her to wish she really were Shelly Lane, physical therapist, free to ask Matt for that kiss.

Chapter Thirteen

Lenora watched as Billy Mack got out of his new red pickup and sauntered toward the front porch of the big house. She wasn't surprised to see him, even though twilight was about to fade to full darkness.

She rearranged her skirt, but kept her right foot tucked beneath it. She was too weary to stand and welcome him like a legitimate guest. Not that he was one. During the years since their respective spouses had died, they'd depended on each other too much to stand on ceremony. Besides, Chideaux was nestled comfortably in her lap.

"Using Kali's dog to practice up for the new grandbaby?" he teased as he dropped onto the swing beside her.

"I don't need practice. My arms have been ready for another grandchild ever since David and Derrick grew too big for me to hold and cuddle. But I think Chideaux misses Kali and Zach."

"As do you," he said. "And don't go denying you aren't ready for your youngest son to come home."

"More than ready. Did you hear that he called today? They're flying in late tomorrow. They'll be here for Sunday brunch. I'm making all his favorite breakfast foods, a homecoming celebration of sorts."

"Glad to see you're hanging in there so well with the CIA problems kicking at you like a mad dog."

"I'm not," she admitted. "I'm just doing a good job of pretending. I have to think this too will pass. I know none of my sons have done anything wrong. They're too much like their dad."

"Yep. Good genes from you and Randolph. How could they miss?"

"And there is one bright spot, other than that we'll soon have a little one to spoil rotten."

"Let's hear it. I could use some good news."

"You were right. Matt and Shelly Lane have really hit it off."

Billy Mack's eyebrows arched. "Did he tell you that?"

"He didn't have to. I see it in their eyes when they're together."

"Don't push too much. You know how scared Matt's always been of the L word."

"Only because he's never been in love before. The real thing doesn't come around that often."

"Shhh." She nodded toward the worn path that circled the house. "There's Shelly. I was hoping she was with Matt, but she must have gone for a walk alone."

"Walking instead of spooning. I know that disappoints you."

"You're showing your age, Billy Mack. Young people don't spoon anymore, at least not the way you meant it."

"They still do it. They just call it something different."

Shelly joined them on the porch and Billy Mack jumped up to give her his seat.

"You stay right where you are," she said. "I'll take the top step so that I can stretch out." Instead, she leaned against the support post and hugged her knees to her chest.

"I don't know if I thanked you properly for driving Jeremiah into town today," Lenora said. "I know that's above and beyond your job description and you're not even officially on duty yet."

"I didn't mind. It gave us a chance to talk. I think he may be warming up to me."

"I'm sure he is. Melvin said the two of you had coffee as well."

"We did."

"He's a nice guy. We all lucked out when Jeremiah brought him into the business and into the family."

Billy Mack nodded in agreement. "For a cantankerous old fart, he has a lot of friends. Melvin was the son of somebody from his past."

"Did Jeremiah talk much about our problems with the CIA?" Lenora asked.

"Some. Mostly he talked about his late wife. He was in a very melancholy mood."

Lenora leaned back and let her mind unleash old memories. "Corrine was the love of his life."

"He said it was love at first sight."

"I'm sure it was, though you wouldn't have always known that by the way he bellowed when things didn't go his way. But we saw a different side of him when she was diagnosed with cancer."

"It's never easy for a man to watch the woman he loves suffer," Billy Mack said. "But Jeremiah took it as hard as any man I've ever seen. I remember that his wife had a private nurse who lived here in the big house. Jeremiah fired her a month before Corrine died, said he wanted to take care of his wife himself. He hardly left her side after that."

"You remember that better than I do," Lenora admitted.

"You'd been storked, and you already had three little ones to care for."

"You have a good memory."

"Yep. Remember things that happened decades ago. Starting to have trouble with what happened yesterday. I remember that nurse was a looker, though. What was her name? Helen, Ellen, Louella, something like that. Anyway, she was mighty riled when Jeremiah up and fired her."

"Jeremiah did right by Corrine and that's all that matters. Love that goes against the odds. It's the heritage of Jack's Bluff."

"And here we go again," Billy Mack said. He reached over and patted Lenora's hand. "I've heard the legend of Jack's Bluff before and I hear a beer in the kitchen calling my name."

Shelly stretched her legs in front of her and toed her way out of her tennis shoes as if she planned to sit awhile. "Matt mentioned there was a story behind the ranch's name, and he said you told it better than anyone."

"Does that mean you want to hear it?"

"I'd love to."

A DOZEN FIREFLIES danced in the growing darkness and the shrill chorus of a thousand tree frogs wafted through the night air. Shelly stared at Lenora and imagined her sitting in that same swing on hundreds of nights like this while her children grew up around her.

Such roots, a continuance that spanned generations. Tonight their lives were full of anxiety and chaos, and still the family had all gathered at the big house like it was the center of their universe. But what would happen when the arrest warrant was issued and at least one of them was handcuffed and carried off to jail?

The thought pulled at her heart like ribbons of steel. Still, she wanted to hear Lenora's story.

"I'll give you the short version," Lenora said, "or we'll never get to bed tonight. Jeremiah's great-grandfather, Calvin Collingsworth, was a commoner in England who fell in love with a woman betrothed to royalty."

Lenora slowed the movement of the swing and smiled. "Betrothed, don't you love that word? It has such a romantic flavor. Nonetheless, the betrothal was not a match made in heaven as the woman fell madly in love with Calvin."

"Sounds like a fairy tale. No wonder you love telling it."

"All except this part where the fairy tale lovers got caught and Calvin went to prison. I'm not sure what happened to his beloved at that point, but when Calvin broke out of prison a few months later, he went back for her and they set sail for America."

"What year was that?" Shelly asked, firmly caught up in the story.

"Eighteen ninety. When ships were not the luxury cruisers they are today. They survived the storm-tossed crossing and landed penniless in the land of opportunity. Calvin decided to make his luck at the gambling tables and won a ranch while playing poker one night in a rough-and-tumble Mississippi River town. He won on a bluff, holding just a pair of Jacks."

"Thus, Jack's Bluff," Shelly said. "Luck was definitely a lady to him."

"Except the ranch wasn't what it is today. It was just a few acres of uncleared land. Most of his neighbors were raising cotton, but Calvin began raising cattle and buying up every scrap of adjoining land that he could. Then in 1920, oil was discovered on the land, and the rest is history. But it's not the oil that makes Jack's Bluff magical. It was that Calvin followed his heart. Just like everyone in the family has from that day to this. Like I did, when I married Randolph."

Lenora's voiced choked on the last sentence, the first indication of how difficult things were for her right now.

"I can see how true love can make a real difference in a person's life," Shelly said, her own feelings for Matt riding much too close to the surface.

"It makes all the difference, Shelly. When you find it, fight for it. Never let it go."

That wasn't an option for Shelly, not now, not even if Matt felt the same way about her as she did about him. But she was going to fight to the bitter end to see that justice was done, even though she was convinced it meant switching sides in the middle of the battle.

Not that she didn't love the agency and all that it stood for. She did. But this time they were wrong.

Chideaux woke up and started to wiggle. Lenora set him on the porch. He stretched and wandered over to Shelly.

Lenora slowed the creaking swing. "Care to join me in the kitchen for a cup of hot tea?"

"Thanks, but I have a few personal things to take care of in my room." Things like trying to make sense of the few facts she possessed, so that she had at least a chance of convincing Brady Owens to hold off on pressing formal charges. It was a long shot at best.

Sort of like winning a ranch with nothing but a pair of Jacks.

"MELVIN ROGERS WAS HIRED on at the management level, even though he'd had no higher level management experience."

"That's interesting," Shelly said, making notes as she listened to Maddie Gatlin's research findings. "But not surprising, now that I've been around the Collingsworths. I can see them going out on a limb and giving a friend's son a chance, if they thought he had potential."

"And he was heavy on potential. A court-ordered psychiatry report when he was thirteen said his intelligence was near genius level. But then it also said he had aggressive tendencies."

"What prompted the court order?"

"Melvin made threats against some boys in his seventh-grade class."

"What kind of threats?"

"He told them he was going to blow up their houses while they were asleep. The court decided it was an idle threat and let him off, as long as he attended counseling sessions for three months."

"What other problems has he had?"

"That's all the bad I could find. On the positive side, he graduated from UT with a double degree in computer science and mathematics."

"So he finally put his intelligence to work. Maybe that's why Jeremiah decided he had potential."

Shelly had been on the phone with Maddie for the past half hour. Maddie had dug up everything she could find on Melvin, but there was nothing to suggest he had reason to frame the Collingsworths.

On the contrary, he had everything to gain by their continued success. He was a vice-president and treated like family. It didn't get much better than that.

"I don't know what you're trying to prove, Shelly, but I think you're hitting a dead end on the Melvin Rogers track."

"You could be right."

"I heard the case was all but closed anyway, that they already have enough evidence to arrest the four Collingsworth brothers."

The air rushed from Shelly's lungs, leaving a horrid burning sensation in her throat. "Are you sure?"

"I heard it from Cates. He's usually pretty reliable."

"But you heard they were arresting all four brothers?"

"That's the story I got."

This was not the development Shelly wanted to hear. "I'll try to get Brady. I need to know exactly what's going on."

"I suspect he's ready to pull you and Ben Hartmann out of there. Oh, but there was one other thing. You asked about Melvin's parents."

"Right. Were you able to find out anything about them?"

"His mother was named Ellie, maiden name, Mellinger. His father was Gabe Rogers. She divorced him when Melvin was twelve years old."

"About the time Melvin was making threats in school. Did she remarry?"

"No, she went back to school to brush up on her nursing skills and went to work at a hospital in Dallas, Texas. That's where she and Gabe had lived for most of their married life. She died six years ago."

"Supposedly one of his parents was a friend of Jeremiah's. I'm not sure which." Shelly thanked Maddie and put in the call to Brady. She got his answering machine and left him a message that she needed to talk to him ASAP. He was probably home with his family, celebrating the upcoming arrests that he'd been dying to make for over a year.

Brady returned her call an hour later. She grew nauseous as he talked, and her stomach retched to the point she could barely stay on the line.

"Ben finally hacked into the right files," Brady explained. "It's all there. Records of money transfers that exactly match the information we'd gotten from our double agents."

"Did you determine which individual actually made the transfers?"

"No, but every member of the family over twenty-one

owns equal parts of the company. That means every member of the family will face charges."

"There has to be some mistake. I've lived with these people, Brady. I know that they are not capable of such an act."

"You've lived with them exactly one week, and not the best week of your life. The mistake was mine in leaving you on assignment after you were shot at last week. A trauma like that can throw off even an experienced agent's judgment."

And he considered her extremely inexperienced. "My judgment wasn't affected," she insisted.

"Then you weren't ready for the case to begin with. I know you don't want to hear this right now, Shelly, but you may not be cut out to be an undercover agent. That's not to say you can't find your niche with the agency."

That was the least of her worries at this point. "Can't you even consider my theory that someone faked the evidence against Collingsworth Oil? Think of the bad press the agency will be in for if you wrongly arrest four members of a family with this kind of clout. They dine with presidents. Their philanthropy in the Houston area is infamous."

"You're out of line, Shelly. I want you off the ranch tomorrow and back in the D.C. office on Monday morning for a debriefing. Tell the Collingsworths you have a family emergency and make whatever flight arrangements you need to make. Put it all on your expense account."

She swayed as the room began to spin. The wheels were in motion; nothing she could say or do could stop Brady's team from running over this family—who she knew was innocent—and smashing them into the dirt.

She should leave the ranch now, spare herself the agony of facing Matt and Lenora and their friends at the benefit tonight. But she wouldn't give up until she had to. She had twenty-four hours left to stop this travesty before Matt and his brothers went to jail.

SHELLY STOOD OVER HER BED, dressed only in a pair of silky thongs as she considered the irony of the situation. She was going to the gala with Matt, wearing Jaime's ball gown and Becky's silver sandals. She'd look great. She'd feel like Judas.

She wasn't even sure why she was going. Her nobler self insisted it was because there was a chance she'd learn some vital piece of information that might help the Collingsworth's defense. Her earthier self knew that it was at least in part because she wanted this one night with Matt before the attraction he felt for her turned to loathing.

She raised her arms and, careful not to muss her makeup, let the emerald silk ball gown slide over her head and down her body. A tingle danced along her spine as the fabric brushed her nipples and embraced her hips.

She'd slipped her right foot into one of the sexy sandals when someone knocked on her door. No doubt Jaime, coming to see if she passed scrutiny.

Shelly pushed her left foot into the other shoe and reached for the borrowed necklace. "Come in," she called, "but close your eyes until I'm fully ready to wow you."

The door opened. It wasn't Jaime. It was Matt. In a black tux and looking so handsome that it literally hurt to look at him. Her mouth went dry and her stomach rolled like the Atlantic Ocean in a hurricane.

"Wow!" he whispered.

A blush heated her cheeks. "I thought you were Jamie."

"The wow still stands. Need some help with that?"

She nodded and held it in place as he stepped behind her and took the necklace from her trembling fingers. Once the clasp was fastened, he put his hands on her shoulders and turned her around to face him. "You're stunning, Shelly."

"It's the dress."

"It's you."

She'd never thought of what it would be like to have someone ravage her body, but she hungered for it now. Tonight would test her mettle, as it had never been tested before. Her only hope of not ending up in his arms was to make certain they were never alone.

"We should go downstairs and meet your mother," she said."

"There's been a slight change of plans. Mom has a raging headache and she's begged off. I'm afraid you're stuck with me for the entire evening."

He leaned closer so that his lips were only inches from hers. Whatever existed between had become a tangible entity that sucked the oxygen from the room and left her mind and emotions so conflicted she could barely function.

If things were only different. If there were a way to start all over again with him. But there wasn't. They'd already passed the point of no return.

She'd hold on for one more night. Tomorrow she'd walk away from him and Jack's Bluff. End it between them, before they ever had a chance to begin.

Chapter Fourteen

The trip into Houston had been by limousine. Matt explained that he refused to drink and drive and he'd need at least a couple of shots of whiskey to get through any affair where the main topic of conversation wasn't football or cattle. Under other circumstances, riding with him in the back of a luxurious chauffeured vehicle would have been pure thrill. Tonight it had been awkward and strained.

But once they'd stepped inside the magnificent art gallery that was hosting the benefit, it was impossible not to get caught up in the glitter and glam. The front foyer with its dazzling crystal chandelier dangling from the three-story ceiling was the focal point of the affair. Beneath it, a pianist played show tunes on a grand piano atop a revolving stage.

Champagne fountains flowed freely, and exquisite morsels that titillated her taste buds were passed around on silver trays. More impressive yet was the constant parade of designer gowns worn by women of every size and age. Not to mention the diamonds that dangled from their ears and necks and dipped into their cleavage. The men weren't bad, either, all in black tie attire and flaunting their importance and charisma. The crème de la crème of Houston society.

Matt fit in every bit as well as he had in Cutter's Bar and

Grill. His charm defied setting, and though he might prefer talking about football or cattle, so far he'd held his own discussing whatever topic had arisen.

They were chatting with the mayor and his wife, when Melvin Rogers arrived on the scene. Shelly did a double take when she saw who'd walked in with him. None other than her CIA cohort Ben Hartmann. Ben had apparently become a lot more infused in the mainstream of Collingsworth Oil than she'd realized.

Angelique spotted them from across the room and came over to join them. She gushed over Matt, air-kissed the mayor and his wife and finally turned her attention to Shelly. "What a pleasant surprise to run into you here."

"Thanks. It's nice to see you as well. I should also thank you for the sketch. It was extremely accurate."

"Best of all, it produced results," Matt added.

"I'm glad I could help. Have you had a chance to view the art and make your silent bids?" she asked, directing the question to the four of them.

"I bid on your painting," the mayor's wife said. "And on that sculpture by Michael Allen. I have lots of competition for both."

"Push it higher," Angelique said, smiling and waving at someone else who'd caught her eye. "It's all for a good cause."

"Right," the mayor agreed. "The Children's Hospital does tremendous work."

"I guess Shelly and I should view the offerings," Matt said. "I have orders from Mom that I'm to come home with a bright and cheerful painting to hang in the nursery of her soon-to-be-born grandson."

That brought new questions about Matt's family, and it was minutes later before he finally steered her away from the foyer and toward a winding staircase.

"Are you sure this is the right way to the auction?"

"No, but it's the right way to the second-floor balcony. I need more air and less people."

"I thought you were having a good time."

"I like people, just not all crowded into one room."

"Did you see Melvin when he came in?" she asked.

"I caught a glimpse of him. I'm sure we'll run into him again later. We won't have to stay late, though. I only promised Mom we'd make an appearance. The Children's Hospital is one of her pet projects."

"She obviously loves children."

"Does she ever! That's why she's so worried about my not being married as yet. She's afraid she'll miss out on a grandchild."

A sign propped on the bottom step said the second floor rooms were not open to the public that evening. Matt guided her past the sign and to the top of the second floor. The balcony opened off a circular room to their right.

The quietness of the night and the beauty of the star-studded sky wrapped around them the second they stepped from the confines of the building. She vacillated between fear and hope that he'd make a sexual advance.

He didn't. Instead he walked to the railing and leaned against it, staring into space.

She stayed a step behind him. "Is something wrong?"

"Pretty much everything."

"Does this have to do with the meeting you had at Collingsworth Oil today?"

"Exactly. I know Jeremiah told you something of the problems with the CIA. I think you should know the rest."

"You don't have to explain your private life to me."

"I know that, but I'd like you to hear my side of the story before you get a twisted version from the news media."

So he knew the warrants were imminent. That made sense. Brady would have had the field agents tighten the noose in hopes of a full confession. Guilt and regret balled in her chest, squeezing her heart until it felt like it might fly into a million jagged fragments.

"The CIA believes our family has committed a heinous crime," Matt continued.

She listened while he explained what she already knew, hating that she was forced to remain in her covert role while he bared his soul. But she'd taken an oath. She couldn't dishonor that as long as she still worked for the CIA.

"The CIA is insisting we cooperate with them, but their view of cooperation is that we admit fault. We can't do that. Not one of us would ever stoop to dealing with terrorists, no matter what they offered in return. But it looks as if someone inside the company may have done just that."

She hadn't expected that admission from him. "What makes you think that?"

"Large sums of money are missing from the company's foreign bank accounts."

"Why do you have foreign bank accounts?"

"Sometimes it makes it easier to do business in the global market."

"How long have you known about the missing money?"

"Since yesterday. Langston hired a private accounting firm that specializes in fraud and they discovered it. As yet we don't know exactly how the transactions were made or who they went to, but it certainly leaves the possibility open that the CIA's allegations are valid, even if they're looking at the wrong suspects."

"What will you do?"

"Keep fighting the charges. Hire attorneys. Make bail if that's an option."

His shoulders drooped beneath the weight of the issues. She stepped closer and he reached out to her, tugging her into the crook of his arm. She relaxed against him, knowing only that she couldn't turn away when he needed her.

"I'm pretty sure we're being framed," he said. "It's the only rational explanation."

"What's the motivation?" she asked, voicing the question that haunted her.

"That's the conundrum. Anytime you have wealth or influence in economic circles, you make enemies. But this would have to be someone on the inside, someone who could finagle the records and cover up so well that the company's accountants never picked it up. Someone we trust."

Someone like Melvin Rogers. Not that she had any real reason to suspect him, other than her instincts and the fact that he rubbed her the wrong way. "Do you have any idea who might be behind this?"

"No one we can all agree on. And we don't want to make unfounded accusations."

"You need to look for motivation. That's the key."

"You sound like Langston's homicide-detective friend."

"It's my *CSI* addiction," she lied.

But motivation was the key, and she couldn't possibly see how destroying the Collingsworths would do anything for Melvin except shut down the gold mine he'd lucked into.

Matt's cell phone jangled and he pulled it from his pocket, checking the digital readout for caller ID. "I need to take this," he said.

She nodded and backed away. "I'll wait inside."

She found a spot at the top of the stairs where she had a good view of the party going on below. She spotted Ben almost immediately. He'd hooked up with Angelique and was obviously enjoying himself. He'd definitely adjusted well to the lifestyle his undercover job provided. But then, who was she to talk when she was here with Matt Collingsworth?

She watched until Angelique was approached by a distinguished-looking gentleman and Ben wandered off by himself. Leaving her post, she hurried down the stairs hoping to catch up with him before he joined a new group of people.

She had a few questions for him that she'd like to ask in person. And this was the one place she could get by with that. She walked off in the direction he'd disappeared. No sign of him in the first viewing gallery, so she meandered the hallway, peeking into each room.

When she'd reached the end of the central hallway without spotting him, she decided to go back to the stairs and wait for Matt before she became separated from him as well. She'd started in that direction when she heard her name called. She spun around to find Melvin only steps away.

"We meet again," he said, a taunting jeer that set her nerves on edge.

"Yes, I saw you when you came in with a friend."

"Ben's not exactly a friend." He stepped closer and leaned into her space. "But then you'd know that, wouldn't you?"

"I don't know what you're talking about."

"Don't be coy, Shelly. We need to talk—alone."

"What about?"

"The reason you're really in Texas."

He knew. And if he did, the information had to have come from Ben. Anger shot through her. Had Ben let it slip accidentally, or could he have been sucked into some bizarre scheme? She had to find out what Melvin knew.

"There's an empty room upstairs," she said, wondering how they'd avoid running into Matt before she had a chance to find out what was going on.

"There's one much closer. At the end of the hallway."

Possibilities bombarded her mind as she followed him down a second hallway, one with dimmer lights and no doors but one opening off it. She grew instantly wary, "We'll talk upstairs or nowhere," she said. "Your call."

"Right. My call."

She turned as a needle plunged into her arm and a painful sting hit her bloodstream. Trying to break free, she swung her elbows, trying to pound him in his chest, but the drug he'd shot into her had already drained her strength and affected her agility.

She moved in slow motion, stretching her neck to search for someone to call to. But the narrow hallway they'd taken had veered from the main section of the gallery. There was no one in sight.

She tried to scream. Melvin's hand covered her mouth. And then he shoved her through the doorway and into a dark alley. She heard the screech of a cat and the engine of a car idling mere feet from where they were standing.

"Nice broad," someone said in a voice that seemed to be coming from under water. She struggled to focus, but the alley was fading in and out and getting blurrier by the second.

"No mistakes," Melvin said. "Follow my orders to the letter."

"Don't worry. You're not dealing with a dope like Frankie. Short of blowing someone up, he never got it right."

"Just get the job done or you'll end up like him."

Her limbs had gone numb, but she knew she was being dragged down the shadowed alley. Her head banged against something hard. She felt herself falling. She never felt herself stop.

MATT FINISHED HIS CALL and went in search of Shelly. He hadn't meant to talk so long, but that had been Zach. He'd just landed at the airport and wanted a full report on the latest developments.

Matt was ready to head back to the ranch. He planned to do that as soon as he found Shelly. He'd ask Angelique to choose a picture and make sure he won the bid. That would satisfy his mother without his being stuck here all night.

He ran into the mayor's wife at the foot of the stairs. "Have you seen Shelly?"

"Yes. Heading that way." She nodded to the narrow hallway to the left of the auction area.

"Was she by herself?"

"No, she was with a young man. They were walking quickly. I thought she might be looking for you. She seems very nice, Matt."

Yeah. Real nice. And she'd vanished.

Unexpected dread tied knots in his ragged nerves as he hurried in the direction the mayor's wife had indicated. He was likely overreacting, but it had only been a week since Frankie Dawson had tried to kill her. Then someone had murdered him.

Nothing made sense these days. So how could anyone know for certain the violence against Shelly had been random? He'd been to enough functions at this galley that he knew that the door at the end of this hallway opened into an alley. He ran the last few yards and pushed through the door.

No one was there. Only one silver sandal. One that Shelly had been wearing. His heart slammed into his chest as a wave of adrenaline rushed his bloodstream. He scanned the alley in time to see a car rounding the corner at breakneck speed.

Déjà vu. Only this time Shelly was most likely in the escaping car. By the time he ran to the front of the building and located his limo, the abductor's car would be long gone.

A truck turned the corner nearest him and rumbled to a stop. The painted sign on the side said Maurice's Catering. It should have read Heaven Sent.

Matt raced to the car, opened the door and yanked the man from behind the wheel. "Sorry, but a woman's been abducted."

The man stumbled away from the car as Matt jumped in and gunned the engine. He never looked back. Somehow he had to find that car. He had to find Shelly—before it was too late.

Miraculously, he spotted what he thought was the abductor's vehicle two blocks in front of him, speeding through a yellow light. Matt swerved in front of another car and pressed the accelerator to the floorboard, slowing just enough at the red light to make sure he didn't crash before speeding though the intersection.

The car turned at the next corner. Matt made the same turn. He was catching up. And this was familiar territory, only a block from Collingsworth Oil. A new fear collided with the terror already building inside him.

Was there some way her abduction could be connected to the problems with the CIA? Surely not.

A pedestrian stepped off the curb in front of Matt. He barely saw the man in time to throw on his brakes and skid around him. As he did, the catering truck shaved the side of a car parked on the street, slowing him down even more. When he reached the corner, the car he'd been following had disappeared.

His spirits plunged. He couldn't give up, but he was driving blindly now with no clue which way the car had gone. The Interstate was only a few blocks to the east. If the driver had taken it, Matt wouldn't have a chance in hell of locating the car by himself.

He grabbed his cell phone and punched Langston's number. His brothers could always be counted on in a crunch. Only, this time, even they might not be able to help. Still, it was worth a try.

SHELLY OPENED HER EYES. Images and shadows swam in a blurry soup in front of her. She felt sick. Her arm throbbed. Her head felt as if it had been used for a basketball. The rest of her was numb.

She drifted in and out of the fog until her mind began to clear in haphazard spurts of memory. Her and Matt standing on a balcony. Following Ben. Talking to Melvin. Jaime's friend, the cowboy from Cutter's Bar and Grill.

Her stomach retched as the pieces began to slide into place. Melvin had led her into a trap. Ben had to have told him who she was. He and Ben were in this together. But why? What could they possibly gain by abducting her?

Ransom money from Matt? Had both of them been seduced by the Collingsworth's wealth? Could they have wanted it badly enough to sink to this?

Burning sensations prickled her body as sensitivity begin to return to her arms and legs. She was being half carried, half dragged by someone with strong hands and muscular arms. Leland. He'd been waiting for her in the alley.

Her vision improved to the point she could tell they were in a darkened hallway with only a glimmer of light. She tried to move her hands and finally realized her wrists and her ankles were bound.

Her feet banged against something hard and then she was dropped to the floor. A light came on, the glare burning her eyes and temporarily blinding her.

When her pupils adjusted, she looked up and into the sneering face of Leland Adams. She scanned the area around her, shocked to find that they were in Lenora Collingsworth's office. Pictures of Lenora's family stared down at her from the tall bookcases.

Shelly's gaze fastened on one of Matt and a new resolve pushed strength into her drug-weakened muscles.

"You won't get away with this, Leland." Her tongue was thick, but her mind had gained a semblance of clarity. "Matt won't pay a ransom for my return. I'm just a lowly family employee."

"A ransom?" He laughed as if this was all a joke. "Honey, you aren't going to live long enough for me to collect a payoff. You're seconds away from eating a bullet. I'd think you'd taste it by now."

The metallic taste of fear clogged her throat. "Why here, Leland? Why bring me to Collingsworth Oil? Why not kill me in the alleyway where Melvin dumped me?"

"I just follow orders, sweetie."

"Melvin's orders."

"What do you care? You're dead no matter who's picking up my tab. But don't worry, I don't plan to leave you here. We're just planting murder evidence."

Evidence to make it look like the Collingsworths had killed her and disposed of the body. As soon as Brady discovered that she was missing, he'd see that they were the first people investigated. Her blood and other evidence of the murder would be found in the hallway and in Lenora's office.

Melvin had thought of everything. The final crush in destroying the Collingsworths. The only remaining question was *why* he hated them so much.

She worked frantically to free her hands, her only chance to fight back. Leland pulled a pistol from his waist and pointed it at her head.

Her blood ran cold, but she refused to go down without a

Joanna Wayne 183

struggle. *The mind was a powerful weapon in itself. Keep the attacker talking. Make him doubt himself.* Strategies she'd learned in her training program fixed themselves in her mind.

"How much is Melvin paying you to kill me?"

"Enough."

"And then he'll kill you, just like he killed Frankie Dawson."

"Shut up, you bitch."

But she had his attention. His right hand was still holding the pistol, but his finger had eased away from the trigger.

"He killed Frankie because he screwed up the job. I won't."

"He killed Frankie because he couldn't risk his squealing on him one day. He'll kill you for the same reason. No real risk to himself in doing it. Killing riffraff off the street is easy. No one ever gets arrested for that. No one really cares."

"He won't be worried about me. I'll be long gone, living like a friggin' millionaire in Mexico."

But sweat had popped out on his brow and was wetting his underarms. Good signs that she was pushing the right buttons.

"You could be as wealthy as you want, Leland. All you have to do is call Matt Collingsworth right now and ask him for ransom. A million or two is nothing to him. His family has billions."

"You already said he wouldn't pay a ransom, you crazy bitch."

"You have nothing to lose by trying."

A nervous tic attacked the muscles in his face, and he put one hand up to try and stop the twitching. His trigger finger was none too steady, either, but it was back in position. She had to do something fast or she'd never live to walk out of this room.

She didn't want to die. Not this way. Not now. Not before

she'd had a chance to have a family of her own. She'd never been sure she wanted that until now when she felt the possibility slipping away. Or maybe it was Matt who'd changed her view on life.

"Make the call, Leland. I can give you the number. Name your price and see if the Collingsworths will come up with it."

A clanking sound seemed to come from inside the walls or possibly from down the hall.

Leland backed against the desk. "What was that?"

"Probably the cleaning crew," she said. "If you shoot me and run, they'll see you and then they'll find my body and know you killed me," she murmured, grasping at anything that could keep her alive.

"No, the cleaning crew doesn't show up until after midnight. I got lots of time left."

"Sometimes they get here early."

"No, Melvin said midnight for certain, and Melvin doesn't make mistakes."

The noise sounded again, louder this time, as if it were right there in the room with them. Leland started freaking out, the frenzied twitch jerking his face into bizarre contortions. He muttered a string of vile curses and pointed the gun at a spot right between her eyes.

She worked frantically to free her hands. The tape held. But she couldn't just lie here and let him kill her. She stiffened and strained her muscles. But Leland's hand had steadied again and a wild glaze covered his eyes.

There would be no reasoning with him now. She would die before she ever really had a chance to live.

"I love you, Matt," she whispered. She hadn't even been thinking the words, but when her subconscious planted them on her lips, she knew that they were true.

Chapter Fifteen

Gunfire exploded in Matt's head, tearing through his skull like jagged shrapnel. He rushed through the unlocked doors of Collingsworth Oil like a bull out of the chute. Not even slowing to flick a light switch, he raced down the hallway, toward the sound of gunfire and the lone glow at the end of the hall.

Agony rocked through him, hurling questions at him. The same questions that hadn't let up since he'd found Shelly's second shoe near the elevator of the building's parking garage.

Why Shelly? Why here? Why the hell had he wasted time calling for help instead of coming here the second he'd lost sight of the car?

He half expected to crash head-on into whoever had fired the shot, but caution never entered his mind. All he could think of was getting to Shelly.

The light was on in Lenora's office, highlighting the blood splatters on the open door. A guttural cry started deep inside Matt's soul and ripped through his body before echoing around him. He couldn't lose Shelly like this.

He was panting as he thrust into the room. His first glimpse was of a man he'd never see before, writhing in pain and holding one hand over his blood-soaked stomach.

"Matt, you came."

The voice went straight to his heart. His gaze found Shelly. A live, breathing Shelly, curled into a ball beside the massive wood file cabinet. Safe, for now.

But when he looked back to the man, he was no longer clutching his stomach. His bloodied fingers clasped a pistol.

"Make one move, and I'll kill her."

"The hell you will."

Fury erupted inside Matt, and in one swift movement, he kicked the gun from the man's hand and sent it flying to the far corner of the office.

The man spit out a grating groan and his body went limp.

Matt bent over him and checked the pulse in his neck. There was none.

But Matt's own heart was pounding as he crossed the room and wrapped his arms around Shelly, cuddling her in his arms for a second before slicing through the tape that bound her.

"This is all my fault. I should never have left you alone. Some protector I turned out to be."

"You saved my life. I thought he was already dead. I would have never seen the gun."

Matt tried to make sense of the scene. "Who shot him?"

"I rolled into him. He stumbled and dropped the gun. When he tried to catch it, it went off. He was already shaking from a noise in the hall."

"It's the air-conditioning system. Mom complains about it all the time."

"How did you find me, Matt? How did you know to come here?"

His mother would call it a miracle. Jaime would say it was fate. Trish would say it was meant to be. "Instinct," he said. "And your shoes."

She smiled and leaned her head against his shoulder. He wanted to say a million things to her, but all he could do was hold her.

He didn't know how long they sat that way, clinging to each other without saying a word. Either seconds or minutes later, the quiet was broken by the arrival of a half dozen Houston cops. Langston's homicide friend Aidan Jefferies was in the lead.

"Hell of a mess you've made here, Matt." Aidan turned to the body. "Is he dead?"

"Yeah."

"Care to explain what happened?"

Shelly pulled away from Matt. "The man abducted me, but I didn't shoot him—"

"Too bad," Aidan interrupted. "The city might have given you a medal. This guy is wanted for a dozen or more murders in the New Orleans and Houston areas and those are just the ones we know about."

"Then you know him?"

"He's legend. Known as the Popper because he'll pop anybody for a night's drinking money. Also known as Twitch because all his past trips on LSD come back to haunt him. He has as many aliases as Matt here has bulls."

"Melvin Rogers paid him to kill me."

The muscles in Aidan's face pulled into taut lines. "Do you have proof of that?"

"Melvin drugged me himself and then handed me into Leland's hands."

"I'll need a full statement from you, but give me a second to call in a request for the crime scene unit. And, Matt, give Langston a call on his cell phone. He's on his way down here now. The rest of your brothers are likely with him. Never seen brothers stick together like you guys do. Tell them to bring hot coffee—lots of it—and donuts. I got a feeling this is going to be a long night."

Bring it on, Matt thought. He could handle anything now that Shelly was safe.

IT WAS TWO IN THE MORNING when Zach dropped Shelly and Matt off at Matt's place. There had been no mention of her going back to the big house.

He'd said he'd never do anything she didn't want him to do, but as good as she'd felt in his arms tonight, he had to believe she wanted him, too. Maybe not with the same hunger he was feeling right now. He could understand that.

She'd been through a lot over the past few hours. If all she wanted him to do was hold her, he could live with that. What he couldn't handle was falling asleep tonight without her in his bed and in his arms.

He opened the front door and held it while she stepped inside. Her silhouette was outlined in the moonlight and shadows. His sister Becky always said the house lacked a woman's touch. What it had really lacked was Shelly.

Odd that he could be so certain of that in one short week, after years of wondering if he was cut out to be in any long-term relationship. But there wasn't a doubt in his mind. He loved her on a dozen levels, all of them begging for release right now.

"What a night," Shelly said. "And to think it had started out with you telling me I looked stunning."

"You still do." He fit a hand on the back of her neck and let his fingers tangle in her hair. Even that felt good.

"I've ruined Jaime's designer dress and lost both of Becky's expensive silver high-heeled sandals." She put her hand to her neck and caressed the pendant. "I still have the necklace, though."

He wondered if she thought any of that really mattered. "Dresses and shoes can be replaced."

She pulled away from him. "I still don't get it about Melvin. Why would he go to such lengths to hurt your family?"

Matt's frustration swelled. "We went over all of that with the police. The answers will come when we have all the facts."

"He'll be arrested as soon as—"

"Can we please just let it go for tonight, Shelly?"

"I think I'm afraid to."

"You don't have to be afraid anymore. You just have to let the police handle it from here on. Melvin is out of your life, out of all our lives."

"It's not Melvin that frightens me." Her voice was raspy. "It's you. It's us. It's…"

She sounded tormented and that hurt. Was she reading his mind and sensing that it was all he could do not to take her right here and now? She must think he was a heartless monster to want her like this after what she'd had to deal with.

"I'm not going to lie to you, Shelly. I went through hell and back when I found that sandal in the alley and figured you had to have been abducted. Then when I heard that shot, I nearly went berserk. I'm crazy about you and I've never wanted to make love to a woman the way I want you right now."

"Because you don't—"

"Please. Just let me finish and then you can tell me what a jerk I am. I want you so badly it hurts, but I meant what I said the other night. I won't kiss you or undress you or push myself on you in any way until you're ready. So it's all up to you. If you want me, you'll have to let me know."

"Matt."

Her voice was tentative, as if she were about to tell him something that she knew he didn't want to hear.

"It won't change anything if you turn me down, Shelly. I'll still be here in the morning and I'll want you all over again. I won't be closing any doors."

The ripped satin dress made tantalizing swishing whispers as she stepped toward him. Her eyes—deep, forest green pools that he was drowning in—bore into his.

"I want you, Matt. I've wanted you since the day we met." She stretched to her tiptoes and touched her lips to his. The need inside him erupted in a rush of passion. He quit thinking and let his body take over. A man's way, but it was the only way he knew.

THE KISS DEEPENED AND Shelly melted into the thrill of it, her body pressing against Matt's. She'd tried to hold back, knowing she had no right to take his love. But once he'd said how much he wanted her, her resolve was swallowed by her raging, wanton desire.

Tomorrow, she'd be strong. Tomorrow, she'd face the reality of her deception and confess everything to Matt and his family.

Tonight, she needed Matt so much she couldn't bear to turn away. Tonight she'd find sweet fulfillment in his arms.

Matt's tongue invaded her mouth, tasting and tangling and claiming her breath. The kiss undid her, opened her up like a surgeon's scalpel and released emotions that had been locked away all her life.

She whimpered when his mouth left hers, but only because his lips were sweetly tormenting as they seared a path down the column of her neck to the swell of her breasts.

"The dress has to go," he whispered.

He unzipped it with one hand while the other cupped and gently squeezed her left breast. The dress slipped to the floor as Matt fit his lips around her peaked nipple. The feel of his tongue circling her areola had the effect of an exotic aphrodisiac, creating a pooling moistness between her thighs.

She thrust her body against him, and he lifted her from the floor, then let her body ride down his, pressing hard against his erection while a thousand sensations exploded inside her.

And then he lifted her in his arms, carried her to the bedroom and lay her on top of the snow-white quilt.

"Just let me look at you," he whispered as he fit his hands beneath the waistband of her silky thong panties and pulled them over her hips and down her legs.

He stretched out beside her, rising on one elbow so he could watch her reactions as he trailed the fingers of his right hand around her breasts and down the smooth flesh of her stomach. He traced it again, this time letting his fingers slide between her thighs and his thumbs skim the opening to her most intimate crevice.

But she wanted more. She wanted to see and feel him, all of him, without the black tuxedo slacks that he'd looked so devilishly handsome in when the night had first started. She needed to memorize every plane and angle of his face and body so that she could pull them up in a million dreams.

"Your turn to lay back and my turn to undress you," she murmured.

"A man lives for moments like this."

"So does a woman." She hadn't before, but only because she'd never imagined anything could feel this way. She undid the button and zipper and fit her hands beneath the waistband of his trousers and boxers. He made it easy for her, lifting his hips so that the pants would slide past them. She yanked the pants and boxers from his feet and tossed them to the floor.

They were both naked now, lying side by side, the peaks of her nipples brushing his chest. He fit his leg between her thighs, opening her so that the could dip his finger inside her. She ran hot at the gentle thrusts, bathing his finger in her hot juices.

"I can't wait much longer."

She fit her hand around his erection. It was long and hard and pulsing with need. "You don't have to wait. I'm more than ready."

"Should I use protection or are you on the pill?"

"Protection."

He reached in the drawer of the bedside table and pulled out what he needed. "Don't get the wrong idea," he said. "The ones I had were laced with cobwebs. These were optimistically bought with you in mind."

"I didn't ask." But she *had* wondered. The nature of a woman.

Seconds later he raised over her, and this time she spread her legs on her own. He pushed inside her, a quick thrust that set her on fire. She buried her face in the smooth flesh of his shoulder as he thrust over and over, his momentum a growing crescendo.

She'd needed this so badly. Needed Matt with all his strength and all his virility. Needed him now so much her fingers were digging into his back as she thrust against him. She wanted nothing to separate them, not even air. This had to last a lifetime.

Matt thrust again and she cried out as they reached orgasm together, the thrill of it stealing her breath. They held on tight, clinging until the afterglow had taken full hold of them.

"I love you, Shelly. And don't say it back. Not until you're ready. But I've never felt like saying that to a woman before, and I needed to get it out before it exploded inside me."

Tears burned the backs of her eyes. She should have told him the truth. She should have never let things go this far. Should have never let him say 'I love you.'"

"We need to talk, Matt."

"No. I don't want to hear what's causing that strain in your voice. Not tonight."

He was right. They shouldn't tarnish this moment. The bitter truth could wait until morning. She cuddled back in his arms and closed her eyes, though she knew she wouldn't sleep.

"I love you, too, Matt. More than you'll ever know. No matter what happens, remember that."

"WE HAVE TO TALK."

Matt reached for Shelly and pulled her back in his arms. "Didn't anyone ever tell you those are the four words a man dreads hearing most from his woman?"

But he couldn't begin to understand the dread that had settled in her heart. He'd said he loved her. Love was supposed to conquer all. It did in songs and movies. It never had in her mother's life. Maybe that's why Shelly had so little faith that it could work this time in hers.

She pulled away from him and slid her legs over the side of the bed. She was wearing his robe. He was still naked, the bulge beneath the sheet making it obvious he was ready to make love again. She tried to convince herself that he still would be when she was finished.

"This isn't easy for me, Matt, but I have to get it out."

"I don't want to—"

"I'm not who you think I am. I'm not Shelly Lane." There she'd blurted it out and there was no way around it now.

He pushed up on his elbows. "What are you talking about?"

"I'm an undercover agent for the CIA."

He winced as if she'd slapped him. "Keep talking."

She did, but nothing came out right. "The allegations affected national security, Matt. And the evidence was overwhelming. I was doing what my job called for. We've stopped any number of terrorist attacks by gathering this type of information. We've saved lives."

He didn't say a word, but after five minutes of listening to her futile attempts to redeem herself, he turned his back on her and scooted off the other side of the bed.

"I haven't given the CIA anything to use against you," she insisted, desperate now to make him understand. "In fact, I've stressed to my supervisor that none of you could possibly be guilty. After last night's incident, the agency will have to see that I'm right and that Melvin was behind all of this."

He grabbed a pair of jeans from the closet and yanked them on.

"Say something, Matt. Anything. Just don't clam up on me like this."

"What is there to say?" He pulled on a pair of socks from the top dresser drawer. "I don't even know who you are."

"You said that you loved me."

He sat back down on the bed just long enough to shove his feet into a pair of boots. "The keys are in the truck. You can go to the house and pack your things while the family's at church. Be off the ranch before they get back."

"If that's how you want it."

"Feel free to take the truck into town or to the airport. Hell, just take the truck. Payment for your physical-therapy services." He turned and walked away without looking back.

Shelly wrapped her arms around her chest as if that could hold her together. Her heart felt as it someone had squeezed it to mush and left it to rot inside her chest. She'd known all along it would come to this, had told herself that falling in love with Matt could never work—that it would end up tearing her apart.

But how could she not have loved Matt Collingsworth?

SHELLY PLACED THE CALL TO Brady Owens and explained about Melvin and the abduction. He was shocked and admitted that he hadn't heard a word from Ben Hartmann. Not surprising, since Ben was likely still asleep at ten o'clock on Sunday morning.

Brady was convinced that Ben would never have revealed her identity. She didn't see any other way Melvin could have found out who she was. But the most important development was that Brady would call off the arrests and start his investigation over based on the new information.

All in a day's work for the CIA.

"I owe you an apology," Brady said once the bulk of the conversation was concluded. "You were dead on with everything, even your suspicions about Melvin Rogers. I dare say there's more to that than we've uncovered."

"I agree, though I can't even imagine why he'd hate a family who did so much for him."

"Money, a woman or revenge. It always boils down to one of those."

"He didn't keep the money for himself," Shelly said. "That rules out greed."

"So if there's not a woman, that leaves revenge. At any rate, I'd still like to see you in the office Monday morning for a debriefing. And I plan to recommend you for a promotion."

"There's a problem with that."

"The debriefing?"

"No, sir. I can make that. Then I plan to tender my resignation."

"This wouldn't have anything to do with Matt Collingsworth, would it?"

"No, sir." Because Matt Collingsworth was having nothing to do with her. "I just don't think I'm cut out for this line of work."

"What will you do?"

"I'd like to spend some time with my mother and see if we can reconnect." She hadn't fully decided that until the words came out of her mouth, but it was what she wanted to do.

They might never have the perfect mother-daughter relationship, certainly nothing like Lenora had with her children, but she was still Shelly's mother. Shelly should make a stab at understanding her.

"I don't suppose there's anything I can say to change your mind about leaving?"

"No, sir."

"We made a mistake, but we're not the bad guys, Shelly."

"I know. Keeping America safe is one of the most important careers going. It's just not for me."

"We'll talk more Monday."

They'd talk, but her mind was made up. She'd found something here on Jack's Bluff that she wanted and it had nothing to do with the wealth or the prestige. It was family—and love. She'd never get a chance to have that with Matt, but if she was lucky, she'd find it with someone else some day.

That is if she ever got over loving Matt.

THE COLLINGSWORTHS had it all—wealth, influence, family. They did as they pleased, used whomever they pleased, rewarded people only if it suited their purposes. No one knew that better than Melvin Rogers.

Jeremiah Collingsworth had used his mother and then thrown her out as if she were trash under his feet. He'd been all too willing to break his marriage vows while his wife lay dying, but it had been Melvin's mother who'd paid. Melvin might never have known it had he not found and read her diary after she died.

Jeremiah could have married Melvin's mother after his own wife died. Then she'd have never turned to the cruel bastard who'd fathered Melvin. Neither her life nor Melvin's would have been the living hell with him it had become. Melvin would have been Jeremiah's son just as his mother had died believing. He'd be a flesh and blood Collingsworth and not the friend who could sit at the table but never share the name.

Not that it would matter now. Even after he'd worked out everything to the most minute detail, the CIA wouldn't play into his hands. Too bad, especially after he'd figured out so quickly who Ben Hartmann was and had fed him information that would have insured the Collingsworths conviction.

He'd even learned from bugging Ben's apartment that Shelly Lane was CIA. If Frankie Dawson had done what he'd been paid to do, they would have never reached this point. She'd have been dead before she had a chance to be seduced by Matt and the rest of the Collingsworths.

Nonetheless, the Collingsworth dynasty was about to come to an end. Melvin's revenge would be sweet. And deadly. And soon.

No one could stop him now.

SHELLY HAD WAITED UNTIL she was certain everyone had left for church before driving back to the big house for her things.

The thought of facing any of the family with the truth when her heart was in shambles was more than she could deal with. Luckily, no one had skipped the worship service this morning. They had too much to be thankful for.

The traditional Sunday brunch would be a major celebration. Zach and Kali were home from their honeymoon and they were all well on their way to having proof that Melvin had framed them.

The only thing they were losing was a physical therapist who Jeremiah didn't want anyway. And once they'd talked to Matt, they'd feel the same loathing for her that he did.

Luckily she'd managed to get tickets for a four o'clock flight from Houston to Dulles. An airport service was sending a car to the gates of Jack's Bluff Ranch. She'd wait there, parked in Matt's truck, out of sight in case her transportation didn't arrive before they returned.

She trudged down the steps from her former guest suite, lugging her two suitcases. Her handbag and carrying case were slung over her left shoulder. The muscles in her wounded right arm were acting out today, a painful reminder of last night's rough and tumble treatment. The least of her present concerns.

She looked back at the house only once as she drove away. She didn't need reminders. The memories of the house and the Collingsworth family were firmly planted in her mind.

Choosing a protected spot just off the road and beneath a cluster of pine trees, she parked the truck and waited. And waited. And waited. At ten before twelve, she called the car service. They'd been held up behind a six-car pileup on Interstate 45, but they were moving now and should be there shortly.

The Collingsworth convoy began driving in at twelve. No one noticed Matt's truck or her. At twelve-forty, her ride had still not arrived. The family would be gathered at the huge dining room table by now.

One of the brothers would say grace. Maybe Matt. Jeremiah would be banging his cane for someone to pass the biscuits. Lenora would be bustling around making sure the serving dishes were full. The twins would be plotting mischief. Trish would be eating for two.

Put it behind you, ex-CIA lady, before you start boohooing all over your travel clothes.

Two blasts of a honk snapped her back to her senses. Her ride had arrived. She climbed out of the truck and was struggling with her bags when a motorbike flew down the ranch road, skidding to a stop at the gate.

Melvin Rogers. She stared in shock. This should have been the last place he'd show up. He surely knew by now that she'd lived through his paid attempt on her life.

There was no sign he saw her while he waited for the gate to open, but she got a good look at him. He was in ratty jeans and an old T-shirt, unquestionably not Collingsworth Sunday-brunch attire.

The gate opened and he swerved through it, passing her waiting ride and roaring away. She picked up her bags and hurried toward the gate. But even as she stepped across the rattling cattle gate, she couldn't shake Melvin from her mind.

What could have possibly drawn him back here when he knew everyone was gathered and that he was a wanted man.

Revenge.

Brady's word came back to haunt her. But revenge for what? It wasn't as if he were a bastard brother or the black sheep of the family. He was just a guy Jeremiah had brought into the fold and given a great job to.

The driver stored her bags and opened the door for her. "Is it just you?"

"Just me," she said.

"Where to?"

"IAH."

"What time's your flight?"

"Not for hours."

"Good thing you gave yourself plenty of time or you'd never have made it. There was a hell of a wreck on I-45. Gas tank on an eighteen-wheeler caught fire in the crash, and before the fireman could get it put out, the whole truck blew like a fire in a fireworks plant. I'm sure it's still smoking. You'll be able to see it when we go by on the other side of the interstate."

Explosions everywhere. Frankie Dawson, known for his explosive prowess. Hired to get rid of her. And Melvin, kicked out of school for threatening to blow the houses of his friends. For revenge? For not being included when he thought he should have been?

Oh, God. That was it. Melvin was almost family, but not quite, because Jeremiah had an indiscretion that he'd never forgiven himself for. With the nurse he'd fired, leaving him to take care of his ailing wife on his own. But the nurse wasn't Ellen, or Helen or Helene. It was Ellie. Ellie Mellinger Rogers.

Melvin's plan to frame the Collingsworth family hadn't worked, but he had an ace in the hole. He'd come back to the ranch this morning to blow them to smithereens.

He was going to prison anyway. He had to know that. He had nothing more to lose and this was his last chance for revenge.

"Turn around. Take me back to the ranch."

The driver looked at her image through his rearview mirror. "What'd you forget?"

"Nothing, but hurry. As fast as you can."

"You sound as if this is life or death."

"It could be." She tried to get Matt on his cell phone. It rang, but he didn't answer. Neither did the phone at the big house. They always let the answering machine pick up during meals.

"Should I wait?" The driver asked as she jumped out of the car.

"No." She used Matt's code to open the gate and raced toward his truck.

"What about your luggage?" the driver called after her.

"Toss it out. I'll get it later." She jumped in the truck, started the engine and yanked the gearshift into Reverse.

Bombing the house was unbelievably bizarre, but it made sense in a crazy way. Melvin's devastating and unrequitedly evil attempts to destroy the Collingsworths. His familiarity with explosives and the people who could provide them. His returning to the house today when he was likely bucking for the top of the Texas most-wanted list.

Matt's family would think she was insane. Maybe she was, but if she was right about this, the big house at Jack's Bluff was on the verge of exploding with all the family inside.

The ultimate revenge of a brilliant madman.

Panic roared through her veins as she pushed the truck to its limits, almost turning it over at the last sharp turn. She threw on the brakes practically at the front steps and jumped from the truck. She started yelling the second she pushed through the front door.

"Everybody out of the house! Now! I'll explain later, but you have to hurry. Please, hurry!"

Langston was the first to reach her. "What is it, Shelly?"

"I just saw Melvin speeding away from the ranch. I think he may have planted a bomb. I think the house may be about to explode."

To her surprise, he took her words at face value. He raced back to the dining room with her a step behind.

"There's an emergency," he said, his voice calmer than hers had been, though his tone left no room for argument. "Everyone clear out of the house at once. Stay together and head for the stable. Now!"

Trish grabbed her daughter's arm. "Let's go, Gina. Do what Daddy says." But Trish was eight months pregnant and moving too slowly. Langston picked her up as if she weighed nothing and carried her out of the house. Gina, Becky and the twins followed.

Shelly scanned the room. "Where's Matt?"

"He didn't show up for brunch," Lenora said, fear pummeling her voice as she herded her family out of danger. "We thought he was with you."

Jeremiah started banging his cane. "What's the dadburn commotion about?"

"A fire drill, Grandpa. Now stop your bellowing." Bart scooped the old man out of his chair, threw him over his shoulder and carried him out. Jaclyn was right by his side.

Zach grabbed his mother's arm and the hand of his new bride and ran with them from the house. Jaime linked hands with Shelly. No one stopped to ask questions. No one panicked. They all just cleared the house and ran.

Jaime and Shelly were almost to the stable when David started yelling. "Blackie! Blackie! You gotta come with us, Blackie!"

Becky tried to calm him, but his cries become louder and more frantic. "Lemme go! Lemme go. I gotta save my dog."

Blackie was still near the house, barking at a squirrel that was staring him down from the trunk of an oak tree.

And then Derrick, who had been standing quietly beside his mother, started running back toward the house.

"I'll get him, David. I'll get Blackie for you."

Langston, Bart and Zack all started after him, but Shelly was closest. She reached him first, but not before he had the squirming, barking puppy in hand.

They were almost home free when the bomb blew, shaking the earth and sending fire and wood shooting skyward. She pushed Derrick to the ground and fell on top of him, covering him with her body while Blackie licked her face and hell rained down on her back.

Chapter Sixteen

Matt had been walking for hours, tramping through pastures and wooded areas with no thought for where he was heading. His head was splitting, the pain worse than the day he'd been kicked in the head by that bull over in San Antonio. He'd learned his lesson that day, had given up rodeo competition for good.

Hopefully he'd learned a lesson with Shelly as well. A man might as well take advice from a fool as listen to his heart. He'd suspected from the very first that she was not what she seemed. So why hadn't he stood by his convictions instead of believing every word that had come from her lying mouth?

He couldn't hate her for doing her job. He...

He couldn't hate her at all. That was the problem. He'd believed what he wanted to believe. And last night, when they'd returned to the ranch, it had been him who didn't want to hear what she had to say. He just wanted Shelly.

Heaven help him. He still did.

He looked around to get his bearings. Not surprisingly, he'd ended up near the big house. Stopping at the base of a towering pine, he pushed up his sleeve and checked his watch. Almost one. The family would be having brunch.

He couldn't have forced down a bite of food on a bet. Not until he made up his mind what to do about Shelly. He stepped into a clearing then stopped dead still as the sound of an explosion rattled his brain and shook the ground. He looked up and saw a giant ball of fire leap into the sky above the big house.

His heart flew to his throat and he started running. He didn't stop until he reached the cluster of his family and spotted Shelly being led toward the stable by Langston and Bart. Her face was covered in soot, her blouse torn.

Derrick saw Matt first and ran toward him. "Shelly saved Blackie, Uncle Matt."

"She saved all of us," Langston said. "I'm not sure what will be left of the house, though."

Lenora latched on to Langston's arm and leaned against his shoulder. "Houses can be rebuilt, son. People are all that matter. And we're all alive because of Shelly."

Matt wanted to hear every detail of her bravery, but there would be time for that later. Years and years of time, he hoped. But right now, he just wanted to hold her close until his heart could get used to having love around.

Epilogue

Five months later

The first hint of fall was in the air when Lenora slipped out the back door of her newly restored house and walked swiftly toward the oldest oak tree. She stood there for long seconds, staring at Randolph's tombstone before she finally dropped to the grass. She leaned against the trunk of the tree, curling her legs beneath her full denim skirt.

"The rehearsal and dinner are this evening," she said, talking to him the way she always did. As if he could still hear her voice. As if he needed these visits as much as she did.

"By this time tomorrow, all our sons will be married. I was afraid I might never see this day for Matt, but Shelly took care of that.

"Well, Shelly's not her real name, but she decided it fit, and she loves the way it sounds when Matt says it. She absolutely adores him.

"They're getting married here at the ranch. I wish you could see the house now that all the damaged areas have been rebuilt. I hate to admit it around your father. You know how Jeremiah likes to brag about the house he built. But I love my new kitchen. I have the neatest new appliances. The range practically does all the work. And that dishwasher can clean the dirtiest of pots without anyone having to rinse them first.

"And your sons have proved themselves quite the wood-workers, too. They built a new dining table that looks so much like the old one, you'd hardly know it was new. And the laughter is just as loud when we all gather around it.

"We're getting to be a rather large group now that Langston and Trish have their marvelous baby boy. And did I tell you that Bart's wife Jaclyn is expecting? She positively glows. And Bart is strutting around like the proudest rooster in the pen."

A butterfly landed on Lenora's skirt. She watched it until it flew away, marveling that something that exquisite could have come from a caterpillar. But ugly things had a way of becoming beautiful. Take all that trouble with the CIA. If it hadn't been for that, Matt would never have found the love of his life.

"Melvin's out on bail until his trial," she said, "but your sons and even Jeremiah are certain he's going to prison. It was revenge, just as Shelly said. Not because he was Jeremiah's son as she'd thought at first, but because he wasn't.

"You said something strange was going on when your father fired Corrine's nurse. Well, when the hubbub about Melvin came out, Jeremiah finally came clean with me. Apparently he'd come home drunk one night and he and the nurse did the deed. She'd gotten pregnant shortly after that. She was already in another relationship so she never bothered to find out for sure whose baby she was carrying."

Lenora heard the approach of a vehicle and looked toward the road. It was only Billy Mack's pickup truck, but the first of the real guests would be arriving soon. She needed to get back to the house and change into the dress Jaime had helped her pick out for the occasion.

"To make a long story short, Melvin's mother left notes in her diary that made him think he was Jeremiah's son. Jeremiah thought he could be right, but insisted on a blood test. Turned out he's not Jeremiah's son, but your father hired him anyway.

"No one knows for sure what went wrong at that point, but the word leaking from his defense attorney's office is that Melvin was furious that Jeremiah used his mother and then kicked her out instead of marrying her when Corrine died.

"Billy Mack says it's more likely Melvin was just angry that he missed out on being a Collingsworth by bad luck. And you might like to know that he didn't transfer everything he stole to terrorists, either. He socked a couple of million dollars away in a Swiss bank account in his name."

She rose and brushed bits of leaves and grass from her skirt. "That's about it, except that I'm still a bit worried about our daughter Becky. Those boys of hers need their father and she's just too hardheaded to accept that football is so important to him.

"If you were here, you'd know what to say to her. I don't anymore. And then there's Jaime. I don't see marriage in sight for her, though she does a super job of enjoying life. She's just—well, she's Jaime."

Lenora started to walk away, then stopped and looked back at the lonesome grave. There was nothing to see, though you'd think that part of her heart should be spilled around it somewhere. "I miss you, Randolph. I always will. But then you always knew how much I loved you."

THE BLUE DRESS SHELLY had chosen for the party tonight was laid out on the bed. The black boots Matt had given her for her birthday were ready and waiting. It was her night, hers and Matt's. The last night they'd spend before they became man and wife.

Matt stepped behind her and slipped his arms around her waist. "The party's going to start without us if you don't get dressed."

"I can live with that."

"After your mother flew here just for the occasion. I don't think you'd dare cancel out on her."

"She spent all day talking about her latest breakup. I'm not sure that counts as a visit to share my wedding celebration."

"It's a start."

"Maybe." But Shelly doubted it. She'd tried to connect with her mother, but the relationship wouldn't take. Everybody didn't have the kind of wonderful, caring mother Matt did. That was life. She was learning to accept it.

"My hesitance to go to the party has nothing to do with my mother."

"Is it my family?"

"Heavens no. I love them all. They're the family I always wanted and never had."

"Then it must be me. Cold feet about saying I do tomorrow?"

"Nothing about me is ever cold when you're around, Matt Collingsworth."

"Then what is it?"

She pulled away. She doubted she could say this in a way he'd understand. "I love our life just the way it is. I love the way you kiss me as if you can't get enough of me. I love the way you can't keep your hands off me when we're together. I love the way we make love like there's no tomorrow, and then minutes later, you're ready to do it again."

He pulled her back in his arms. "So what's the problem?"

"I know things will change over time, but I don't think I can bear it if we lose the hunger and passion."

"How could I ever not be hungry for you when I've waited for you all my life?"

He kissed her lips and the thrill of him ran through her like liquid fire. It always did. "But what about later, Matt? What will happen when I no longer excite you?"

"You'll always excite me, even when we're old and gray and so feeble we have to help each other to the bed."

He was half teasing. She wasn't. "Do you promise, Matt?"

"I promise." He tilted her chin so that she had to meet his gaze. "You're not your mother, Shelly. I'm not like the men she's chosen to be with. I've only loved one woman in my life. That's you. And I'll be around to love you 'til death do us part. I wouldn't make a vow I don't plan to keep."

"I guess I did let my issues with my mother creep into the back of my thoughts. A lifetime of not trusting love is hard to get past."

"I'm always going to love you."

"How can you be so sure?"

"Because I know me and I know you. And I know our love is real. Forever and always. We can't miss. Ask my mom. She'll tell you it's the legend of Jack's Bluff."

"She did tell me, but what about Becky? She split up with her husband."

"For now, but she still loves him. They'll find a way to make it work. But just for the record, we're not them, either. You have to trust me, Shelly. You have to trust yourself and trust our love."

"I do trust you. It's just that—"

"No, you either trust me or you don't. Do you believe I love you?"

"Yes." The answer was honest. "But forever is such a long time."

"And I was just thinking it's not nearly long enough."

He kissed her again, and she let the sweet promise of his love wash through her. Forever and always. With Matt. In this place they both loved. Surrounded by family. Held tight by roots of the past and challenges of the future. How could she ask for more than that?

She reached for the blue dress. "Party time."

"Are you sure you're ready, Shelly?"

"I'm positive, Matt Collingsworth."

* * * * *

Look for Becky's story soon!
MIRACLE AT COLTS RUN CROSS
November 2008.

*The editors at Harlequin Blaze have never been afraid
to push the limits—tempting readers with the forbidden,
whetting their appetites with a wide variety of story lines.
But now we're breaking the final barrier—the time barrier.*

*In July, watch for BOUND TO PLEASE by fan favorite
Hope Tarr, Harlequin Blaze's* first ever *historical
romance—a story that's truly Blaze-worthy in every sense.*

Here's a sneak peek...

Brianna stretched out beside Ewan, languid as a cat, and promptly fell asleep. Midday sunshine streamed into the chamber, bathing her lovely, long-limbed body in golden light, the sea-scented breeze wafting inside to dry the damp red-gold tendrils curling about her flushed face. Propping himself up on one elbow, Ewan slid his gaze over her. She looked beautiful and whole, satisfied and sated, and altogether happier than he had so far seen her. A slight smile curved her beautiful lips as though she must be in the midst of a lovely dream. She'd molded her lush, lovely body to his and laid her head in the curve of his shoulder and settled in to sleep beside him. For the longest while he lay there turned toward her, content to watch her sleep, at near perfect peace.

Not wholly perfect, for she had yet to answer his marriage proposal. Still, she wanted to make a baby with him, and Ewan no longer viewed her plan as the travesty he once had.

He wanted children—sons to carry on after him, though a bonny little daughter with flame-colored hair would be nice, too. But he also wanted more than to simply plant his seed and be on his way. He wanted to lie beside Brianna night upon night as she increased, rub soothing unguents into the swell of her belly, knead the ache from her back and make slow, gentle love to her. He wanted to hold his newly born child in his arms and look down into Brianna's tired but radiant face and blot the perspiration from her brow and be a husband to her in every way.

He gave her a gentle nudge. "Brie?"

"Hmmm?"

She rolled onto her side and he captured her against his chest. One arm wrapped about her waist, he bent to her ear and asked, "Do you think we might have just made a baby?"

Her eyes remained closed, but he felt her tense against him. "I don't know. We'll have to wait and see."

He stroked his hand over the flat plane of her belly. "You're so small and tight it's hard to imagine you increasing."

"All women increase no matter how large or small they start out. I may not grow big as a croft, but I'll be big enough, though I have hopes I may not waddle like a duck, at least not too badly."

The reference to his fair-day teasing was not lost on him. He grinned. "Brianna MacLeod grown so large she must sit still for once in her life. I'll need the proof of my own eyes to believe it."

Despite their banter, he felt his spirits dip. Assuming they were so blessed, he wouldn't have the chance to see her thus. By then he would be long gone, restored to his clan according to the sad bargain they'd struck. He opened his mouth to ask her to marry him again and then clamped it closed, not wanting to spoil the moment, but the unspoken words weighed like a millstone on his heart.

The damnable bargain they'd struck was proving to be a devil's pact indeed.

* * * * *

Will these two star-crossed lovers find their
sexily-ever-after?
Find out in BOUND TO PLEASE by Hope Tarr,
available in July
wherever Harlequin® Blaze™ books are sold.

Harlequin Blaze marks new territory with its first historical novel!

For years readers have trusted the Harlequin Blaze series to entertain them with a variety of stories— Now Blaze is breaking down the final barrier— the time barrier!

Welcome to Blaze Historicals—all the sexiness you love in a Blaze novel, all the adventure of a historical romance. It's the best of both worlds!

Don't miss the first book in this exciting new miniseries:

BOUND TO PLEASE
by Hope Tarr

New laird Brianna MacLeod knows she can't protect her land or her people without a man by her side. So what else can she do—she kidnaps one! Only, she doesn't expect to find herself the one enslaved....

Available in July wherever Harlequin books are sold.

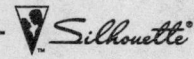

SPECIAL EDITION™

Little did hotel-chain CFO Tom Holloway realize that his new executive assistant spelled trouble. But even though single mom Shelly Winston was planted by Holloway's worst enemy to take him down, Shelly was no dupe—she had a mind of her own and an eye for her handsome boss.

Look for

IN BED WITH THE BOSS

by *USA TODAY* bestselling author
CHRISTINE RIMMER

*Available July
wherever you buy books.*

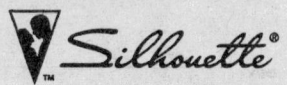

Romantic
SUSPENSE

**Sparked by Danger,
Fueled by Passion.**

Conard County: The Next Generation

When he learns the truth about his father, military man Ethan Parish is determined to reunite with his long-lost family in Wyoming. On his way into town, he clashes with policewoman Connie Halloran, whose captivating beauty entices him. When Connie's daughter is threatened, Ethan must use his military skills to keep her safe. Together they race against time to find the little girl and confront the dangers inherent in family secrets.

Look for

A Soldier's Homecoming

by *New York Times* bestselling author
Rachel Lee

Available in July wherever you buy books.

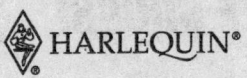

HARLEQUIN®

American ★ Romance®

MADE IN TEXAS

It's the happiest day of Hannah Callahan's life
when she brings her new daughter home to Texas.
And Joe Daugherty would make a perfect father
to complete their unconventional family. But the
world-hopping writer never stays in one place
long enough. Can Joe trust in love enough to
finally get the family he's always wanted?

LOOK FOR

Hannah's Baby

BY

CATHY GILLEN THACKER

*Available July
wherever you buy books.*

LOVE, HOME & HAPPINESS

REQUEST YOUR FREE BOOKS!

2 FREE NOVELS PLUS 2 FREE GIFTS!

Breathtaking Romantic Suspense

YES! Please send me 2 FREE Harlequin Intrigue® novels and my 2 FREE gifts (gifts are worth about $10). After receiving them, if I don't wish to receive any more books, I can return the shipping statement marked "cancel." If I don't cancel, I will receive 6 brand-new novels every month and be billed just $4.24 per book in the U.S. or $4.99 per book in Canada, plus 25¢ shipping and handling per book and applicable taxes, if any*. That's a savings of close to 15% off the cover price! I understand that accepting the 2 free books and gifts places me under no obligation to buy anything. I can always return a shipment and cancel at any time. Even if I never buy another book from Harlequin, the two free books and gifts are mine to keep forever.

182 HDN EEZ7   382 HDN EEZK

Name	(PLEASE PRINT)	
Address		Apt. #
City	State/Prov.	Zip/Postal Code

Signature (if under 18, a parent or guardian must sign)

Mail to the Harlequin Reader Service:
IN U.S.A.: P.O. Box 1867, Buffalo, NY 14240-1867
IN CANADA: P.O. Box 609, Fort Erie, Ontario L2A 5X3

Not valid to current subscribers of Harlequin Intrigue books.

**Want to try two free books from another line?
Call 1-800-873-8635 or visit www.morefreebooks.com.**

* Terms and prices subject to change without notice. N.Y. residents add applicable sales tax. Canadian residents will be charged applicable provincial taxes and GST. Offer not valid in Quebec. This offer is limited to one order per household. All orders subject to approval. Credit or debit balances in a customer's account(s) may be offset by any other outstanding balance owed by or to the customer. Please allow 4 to 6 weeks for delivery. Offer available while quantities last.

Your Privacy: Harlequin is committed to protecting your privacy. Our Privacy Policy is available online at www.eHarlequin.com or upon request from the Reader Service. From time to time we make our lists of customers available to reputable third parties who may have a product or service of interest to you. If you would prefer we not share your name and address, please check here. ☐

HI08R

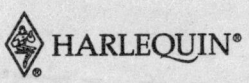

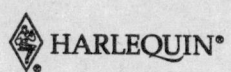

INTRIGUE

COMING NEXT MONTH

#1071 IDENTITY UNKNOWN by Debra Webb
Colby Agency

Sande Williams woke up in the morgue—left for dead, her identity stolen. Only Colby agent Patrick O'Brien can set Sande's life straight, but at what cost does their partnership come?

#1072 SOLDIER CAGED by Rebecca York
43 Light Street

Kept under surveillence in a secret, military bunker, Jonah Baker is a damaged war hero looking for a way out. Sophia Rhodes may be the one doctor he can bend to his will, but their escape is only the first step in stopping this dangerous charade.

#1073 ARMED AND DEVASTATING by Julie Miller
The Precinct: Brotherhood of the Badge

Det. Atticus Kincaid knows more about solving crimes than charming ladies. But he'll do whatever it takes—even turn quiet Brooke Hansford into an irresistible investigator—to solve a very personal murder case, no matter the family secrets it unearths.

#1074 IN THE MANOR WITH THE MILLIONAIRE
by Cassie Miles
The Curse of Raven's Cliff

Madeline Douglas always had dreams of living in the big house. But taking up residence in historic Beacon Manor is the stuff of nightmares, which only the powerful and handsome Blake Monroe can help to overcome.

#1075 QUESTIONING THE HEIRESS by Delores Fossen
The Silver Star of Texas: Cantara Hills Investigation

With three murder victims among her social circle, Caroline Stallings isn't getting invited to many San Antonio events. Texas Ranger Egan Caldwell is the one man returning her calls, only he's spearheading an investigation that may uncover a shared dark past.

#1076 THE LAWMAN'S SECRET SON by Alice Sharpe
Skye Brother Babies

Brady Skye was a disgraced cop working tirelessly to win back his reputation. But only the son he never knew he had can help him piece together his life—and reunite him with his first love, Lara Kirk—before someone takes an eye for an eye.